7

FELONIES

Part 1

One Woman's Journey Of Poor Choices

A Memoir

SHAPELL DEPREE

Published and Distributed by:
Butterfly Soul Publishing
P.O. Box 49653
Greensboro, North Carolina 27419
Email: butterflysoulpublishing@yahoo.com

First printing December 2011
978-0-615-58024-1
10987654321

Table of Contents

Dedication

I would like to dedicate this book to the creator of the universe first and foremost because without him I wouldn't be in existence. I want to thank my wonderful family and friends for their continued support during my life experiences.

I would like to thank the creator for the woman that gave birth to me. My mother Bonnie has been my motivation, inspiration and strength in my most challenging moments. I never would have imagined living my life without this woman and every day has been a struggle. Bonnie has been thoroughly missed during the most trying times throughout my journey. I dedicate this book to my beautiful mother Bonnie, whom I adore and miss every day. There is no love, like a mother's love!

Love,

Always

Acknowledgements

I would like to thank the creator for allowing me to write about my life experiences. My Grandmother Helen on my mother's side is one of the best grandmothers in the world! She makes the best homemade biscuits in town. My Grandmother Helen was blessed with eight healthy children with her husband Leroy. Helen had four boys and four girls. My mother Bonnie was the second youngest of the girls. Helen has always been there for me and my brother Travis whenever we needed her. She did her best to provide for us as she did for her own children. I give special thanks to each one of my Aunties; Debra, Jean and Tama.

I want to thank each of my Uncles; June, Butch, Perry and Lee Lee. I want to thank my uncle and aunties by marriage; Frank, Rita and Karlen. I have been truly blessed to come from such a huge and loving family.

My Grandmother Mary on my father's side is just as wonderful and has been very supportive of me. Mary makes the best pound cakes in town! Mary was blessed with four healthy children with her husband Billy. Mary had three boys and one girl. My Uncles Mac and Jimmy have been there, as well as my Aunt Mary Lynn. I would like to give honor to my father Gary for assisting with bringing me into the world. I love you with all my heart!

Special thanks to my brother Travis, whom I love dearly and wouldn't trade for anything in the world. We have been blessed to be a part of one another's life. I pray that Travis is blessed with all of his heart's desire. Travis is my little, big brother that always wants to make sure his sister is okay and I always want to make sure that he's okay. Travis is my heart, I can't help acting like a mother to him and he can't stand it. Thank you Travis for always looking out for me!

I have several cousins that have been there throughout the years and friends. I give special thanks to Broc, Dana, Kiana, LaTosha, Ronda, Siera, Sheree and Tracey. Thanks to Deon, Freedom, Kemp(Wes), Kim B., Kim F.,

Nilay, Philonda, Po(Annetta), Randi, Sekima, Sherri and Teadra. Thanks to Tonya and my sister Britney for your continued support. Thanks to my brother Rick and his daughter Nia. A special thanks to Ms. Sullivan. My family and friends whom I didn't name, I appreciate each and every one of you personally. I love you more than words can express. I'm thankful for everyone that has touched my life in a special way. The journey through life has required every one of you at some point. I'm grateful that the creator allowed you to be a part of my life!

Last, but not least, I want to thank the creator for allowing an Angel into my life and showing me my gift! Everyone has a distinct purpose for being in someone's life. Thank you for being one of my true friends and being there when I needed you. Now, I understand the importance of time and being patient!

About the Author

Originally, born and raised in Greensboro, North Carolina. Shapell Depree grew up in the projects by the name of Claremont Courts on Phillips Avenue. I lived on Patio Place. My family resides in Greensboro. There are a few family members in other states. The majority lives in Greensboro. I've had every opportunity to move to another state, but never wanted to leave the nest. My mother Bonnie to whom I have dedicated this book had me and my brother Travis. Bonnie only had two children. Me and my brother Travis were her everything. We made her world go round. Nothing was too good for her babies.

My life is different in certain aspects, but I know that many others can relate! Life teaches us the same lessons in different manners. I have enjoyed writing this book and look forward to Part 2 of 7 *Felonies*. I have always enjoyed reading and journalism. When I have extra time, I like to exercise, travel and spend time with the people I love!

I'm a very relaxed individual and I love the simple things in life. A good laugh is always the best medicine for me. Laughter is food for the soul. It's necessary in any relationship to be healthy. I love to have people around me with good, positive energy!

Everyone that knows me, know that I smile all the time. I have a very infectious smile and enjoy smiling. A smile can actually brighten someone's day that wasn't going as planned. I'm a spiritual person and want to help anyone that I can. I don't have to know you to bless you!

I have always wanted to write a book, but wasn't sure of what kind. I didn't even know where to start and here I am today. Writing is like a medicine that can heal the soul. I have written poetry over the years just for fun. My passion for writing has become my newfound love!

Introduction

...*Love* is received and given in so many aspects. We receive love from our parents, family, friends, co-workers and associates as we journey through life. Love has several different meanings to each of us. Once we feel in our heart that we love someone there is no way to prove otherwise. Love isn't chosen many times. The best love comes out of nowhere when we least expect it. We confuse ourselves and before we know it, we think that we are head over heels in love with someone. Ultimately, to have true love for someone is to treat them a certain way. There's no absolute cause and effect to loving someone. Everyone has a different tolerance level with their emotions.

My journey has always been a search for true love. When I look back over the years, I realized that where I've looked has often been in the wrong places. Most people know that love comes and goes, but most would like a love that stays. Love comes from a feeling deep inside and when returned, is expressed with actions. We have to love ourselves before we can offer love to another. I didn't realize what loving "you" meant. My journey through life has taught me just that. I have always been a pleaser to everyone else. My past relationships gave me a reality check with myself. It made me take a look in the mirror at myself and concentrate on loving the most important person—me. Sometimes I feel that I'm in search of a fairy tale, but I continue to wait because it should be. Most females have this very same desire within each of their hearts as a little girl. A fairy tale in a sense is like a dream. Dreams really do come true!

Love

Men have often told me that I'm looking for just that, a fairy tale. When I express the type of thoughts that I have about a relationship, they tend to agree that it's something that doesn't exist. I beg to differ because I can feel that it's out there somewhere in the universe. Typically, children speak of fairy tales. This is what makes it unbelievable coming from an adult. Our thoughts and actions usually are formed from the environment that we are raised in.

Despite the disappointing relationships throughout my life with my family and friends, I have continued to believe that there is someone out there that will love me unconditionally. I have felt at times that I have been denied the true chance at love due to circumstance. Many of my circumstances are due to the choices I made. My desire is to find my soul mate that will reciprocate what I give to him.

My faith keeps me looking forward to a fairy tale type of relationship one day. Faith is an internal force that I faithfully walk by. I believe in true love and with patience it will come. Along with patience you must have spiritual guidance. I believe combining the two will introduce you to unconditional love. A spiritual connection is necessary when combining with the physical. We have no control over whom we love. You can try to change what is in your heart and mind, but true love always wins.

It was the summer of 1988. I was 10 years old. I remember as a child my mother Bonnie and my Aunt Debra took us to Woodmere Park. It was my brother Travis, my cousin Layla and I. The park was down the street from where we lived on Rayston Drive. This is where we moved after living in Claremont. My mom and aunt went back to the house for blankets. We were going to have a picnic that day. They left us at the park momentarily. We were instructed to stay and not leave. This wasn't going to happen. We wanted to venture off like most curious children when left unattended. There was a place in the woods that was a hop and a skip away from the park. I called this place "Marine Land" a place that we always wanted to discover. Marine Land was traveled by many teenagers to Carolina Circle Mall in Greensboro to hang out. It was like another world to me. It was beautiful, peaceful, and serene. It was a made up name in my mind, the place was real and allowed me to escape. Marine Land was covered with trees which made it secluded and hard to find unless you knew it was there. The water ran along the creek and streamed over every rock that seemed to be purposely placed. The rocks within the creek were perfect to jump on. We jumped from rock to rock with hopes of not slipping into the creek. We disappeared into the forest.

We were missing in action long enough to be afraid of what awaited our return. When we made it back to the park our parents were waiting and very upset. They had something in store for us when we made it home. Marine Land was well worth us getting one of the worst whipping's ever. My mother didn't discipline me much because I listened to whatever she said. She would do more talking than striking. When she spoke her mind! You better take heed to it! I always took heed. I was the type of child that would cry if you raised your voice, so I didn't need to be whipped. Better yet, I didn't want one.

I wish all children could grow up with their parents. Having both parents was something I longed for. However, it's up to the creator who is placed in your life, the reason and the lesson you will learn. Also, the amount of time you will have in their presence. There is a difference in children who are raised by both parents. Also, single parent homes, parentless homes and abusive homes will impact a child's transition in life. Normally, people search for love in other people when it has been missing in their life for so long. Typically, it will be a person outside of the family. The search is for the desired love of a parent that was absent in your life while growing up. When love is absent a person will attach to the first person that acts as though they care.

When you meet someone you should be able to learn from them. We are taught lessons from ourselves and others that have been placed in our path. If you don't understand the concept, the universe will give the same situation back to you. You will continue to see the same characteristics until you realize what is being shown to you. We should show mutual respect to others no matter what type of relationship it is. Many times we don't.

Sometimes people are sent into your life again to tell you something you already know. They're telling you something that you are already aware of, but didn't realize it. That's how the universe works. Sometimes it only takes one time before you actually get it. The universe will give you different opportunities with different people. That's one of life's beauties. The universe doesn't give up on you. The universe will give you what you ask for, but be careful. Sometimes we want things and don't realize how we should treat them once we receive them.

Love can be misunderstood and even confusing at times because of the dynamics involved. When we are working on loving ourselves, we tend to bring others into the circle. That can mess everything up. This is what causes arguments and fights in any relationship.

We don't realize, if we love ourselves first,
everything else will fall into place. Our
energy and focus can be misguided when
we give power to others.

Bonnie

When I think back over the years about the first person I shared love with. It was my mother Bonnie. My strong desire for love stems from a dynamic bond between the two of us. It's hard not to love and respect the woman that gave birth to me. I feel as though I never fully experienced the relationship that a mother shares with her daughter. Bonnie was the best mother that any child could ask for. She made sure me and my brother Travis were dressed in warm clothes. My mother Bonnie had food on the table for us. My biggest praise goes to women that are forced to be single mothers. I feel the same way about single fathers. It's not easy doing it alone. Every day my mother would prepare breakfast for our family. During the week, my brother Travis, my cousin Layla and I were sent to the bus stop with a hot sandwich wrapped in foil. Most of the time, we would be the only children standing there with a hot breakfast sandwich.

My brother Travis and I slept with our mother Bonnie up until a couple of years before she passed away. I would be on one side of my mother and my brother would be on the other side. Travis was just as close to our mother. My brother Travis and I could go for twins. We both have a light complexion, light colored eyes, full lips and reddish-brown hair. He's taller than me. At the time I was ten and Travis was seven. Travis is three and a half years younger than me. I have always felt that it affected him more. We had our own room and still wanted to get in the bed with our mother. You can only imagine the bond we shared with her. She was the consistent force in our lives.

I remember when my mother would go out to the club. I would wait up for her. I would sit on the couch in the living room and look out the window until she returned. The couch was positioned in front of the window. My knees were pressed into the cushion of the couch. My arms were propped up on the back of the couch. While my head rested in my hands as I patiently waited. She was probably right up the street at Side Effects. This is where she would party at from time to time.

Honestly, I couldn't sleep until she returned. I needed to know that she had made it home safely. I looked for lights to come down the street in hopes that it was my mother. Once the car pulled into the driveway, I would run and jump into the bed only to pretend that I was sleeping. I would do this any time my mother went out. She never knew that her little girl that was supposed to be sleep in bed was actually waiting for her return.

Sometimes my mother would take me and my brother Travis to our great grandmother's apartment to stay. Great Grandma DeGraffenreidt lived at Gateway Plaza in downtown Greensboro on Spring

Garden Street. It was designed for senior citizens or older adults. My Great Grandmother DeGraffenreidt was my Grandmother Mary's mother. My great grandmother allowed me to have coffee and pancakes. We would stay the night with our great grandmother. I can remember our Great Grandma DeGraffenreidt taking us to the Woolworth's on Elm Street in downtown Greensboro, NC. The Historic Woolworth is significant due to the sit-in that took place there in 1960. The Woolworth's Lunch Counter is now part of the International Civil Rights Center and Museum in Greensboro. Our great grandmother would take all of her grandchildren there for ice cream, coloring books and crayons when they stayed with her. My Cousin Dana remembers getting panties, pretty socks with lace that could be folded down when worn with pretty dresses and ribbons for the hair. Dana remembers having a hot dog, a coke to drink and ice cream. She would buy us school supplies as well. She would spoil each one of her grandchildren whenever she kept us. We looked forward to spending time with our great grandmother. Our great grandmother was in her early 80's and still getting around pretty good for her age. She didn't stop walking to Woolworth's until she was in her early 90's. She lived to be 97 years old.

My mother was a hair stylist and was known for being one of the best at it around town. She attended Leon's Cosmetology School and graduated. She later went on to work for Mr. Dudley. She worked at the Dudley's Center located on South Elm Street in Greensboro. My mother Bonnie could sew a full head of hair onto a person's head that only had a strand of hair. That's how phenomenal she was. I grew up around hair. My mother did hair at home and in a salon. I never had to worry about getting my hair done because I had my very own stylist. I can't say that I liked all of the styles that my mother gave me. I had the style known as the "Jerry Curl" which was the worst style for any child. This style was supposed to be the recipe for damaged hair and was popular in the 80's. Most of the time you had to cut the relaxer out.

That was the case with my hair and I couldn't stand it. My hair was so short that I felt that I looked like a little boy.

In the beginning of my mother's illness, I wanted to run away and never come back. At that time, I wanted to stay away and not see my mother in that condition. I was use to seeing a strong, black, independent woman that had everything together. She had a light blue Gremlin and a red Chevrolet during our childhood years. I remember her playing "Superwoman" in the car by Karyn White.

I had a friend from middle school named Tina. She lived with her father. He wasn't very strict on her at all. Tina's father would let her have company at the age of twelve. I went to Tina's house without permission. After school on a Friday, I rode the school bus home with her. Tina lived in Smoketree apartments on Yanceyville Street in Greensboro, NC. That night we had boys over from school who were allowed to drink and smoke weed if they wanted to. Due to my feelings about my mother being sick, I began to act out. I acted out by making my own decisions. No one in my family knew my whereabouts. I spoke with my cousin Layla by phone who told me that everyone was worried. Layla was four-foot-eight with a black Indian texture of hair that was medium in length and a light brown complexion. I called my Aunt Debra and told her where I was at. I was allowed to spend the night, but I would be picked up first thing in the morning. My Grandmother Helen was taking care of me and my brother Travis during this time. This was the beginning of my many poor choices.

My mother found out that she had cancer at the age of thirty. The first major surgery on my mother traumatized me. The entrance of Moses Cone Hospital had two double doors that opened once you were in front of them. We had to enter more automatic doors once arriving to ICU. The ICU was for people who needed around the clock care or monitoring. There was only a small amount of rooms in this area because of the direct attention required with each patient. It was a place that was huge to me as a child. It appeared dark and gloomy. She was placed in the hospital's ICU and had several tubes hooked up to her. There was no way that a child could tolerate seeing their mother looking so helpless. I was taken in by family to see my mother in recovery. I began screaming immediately and I had to be escorted out of the ICU. I never felt the same after that visit to the hospital. The mere mention of going to the hospital or knowing someone that was hospitalized would give me the chills. My mother had more than one surgery. The cancer began to spread. Chemotherapy was recommended with hopes of stopping the spread of cancer.

During the time my mother was ill, I stayed busy spending time with friends. I would play outside with friends. There was a basketball court in Claremont that most children gathered at. It was right in front of my Grandmother Helen's apartment. We were allowed to play there until the street lights came on. I knew that once the lights came on, it wouldn't be long before being called in by my grandmother.

While my mother Bonnie was living my father would keep in touch by phone. My mother and father met while attending Page High School in Greensboro, NC. My father Gary moved to Atlanta, Georgia before my mother ever knew that she was sick. Gary was five-foot-seven, a brown complexion and wore a close haircut. My father was very smooth and dressed dapper. Gary was a ladies man and knew how to have a good time. He moved to make a better life for himself as a professional chef. He's an amazing cook. Gary came to get us a few times over the summer. He made more of an effort to see us while our mother was living. I remember visiting him twice over the summer. I don't remember much about the trip because I was only seven years old. My father reminded me of how he would sit me on his lap and let me drive. I was a toddler in the late 70's. I remember it vaguely as well as the apartment he lived in when he was dating my mother. It was off of East Market Street in Greensboro near the railroad track next to Sprinkle Gas Station and Lowdermilk Street. During the time that my mother was fighting cancer, she was able to stay at home with the help of family and hospice. My father came to assist my mother during this time. He helped by cooking, cleaning, watching over my brother Travis and I while caring for our mother. At the time, my father had hopes that our mother would recover. My father later found out that my mother's illness was terminal. He couldn't bear the thought of losing her or even watching her fade away slowly.

Some time before my mother became increasingly ill; I asked her if she was going to die. Her response to me was that she didn't know. My mother had an abundance of courage and strength. She only knew that she was willing to fight this battle known as cancer. Her only concern was who would take care of her precious children.

My mother was hospitalized during the last month of her life. I would hear from my family that my mother asked for me day after day. One particular night I was at my friend Carmen's house when hearing that my mother was asking for me. Carmen lived about 2 doors down from me in Claremont Courts. I remember being with her and attending the fun fourth that was held in downtown Greensboro every year. We went with her family to the function. We were dressed alike in our denim shorts. The jean shorts were cut out with holes on the front and black tights extended from underneath them. The tights stopped right above our knees along with black t-shirts and sneakers. We thought we were cute. I would do things to make me feel normal at this time. It took about two days before I came to answer my mother's call. I didn't want to see her in that condition. Neither did my brother Travis. He was hurting just as much. Travis was dealing with the illness of our mother in his own way. I knew that her hours were limited and she wanted to see her little girl one last time. I can't tell you what took me so long. Maybe it just seemed long thinking back. Maybe my mother just wanted to hear my voice. At this point she was constantly and heavily sedated with medication to keep from feeling the pain.

When I arrived at the hospital, it was two days after the 4th of July. My Grandmother Helen and her older sister Patsy were at my mother's bedside. I immediately went to her and grabbed her hand. I began telling my mother that I was there. I knew that she was sedated, but could hear my sweet voice.

My visit at the hospital that night was brief and my mother didn't wake up to see me as I spoke to her. I started out the door and was saying bye to my mother. The entire time I looked at my mother lying on her sick bed hoping that she would open her eyes. I knew that she wasn't fully conscience and could hear me if nothing else. My mother woke up briefly and lifted her hand to wave goodbye to me one last time before I reached the doorway. It was years later before I realized the significance of that very moment—a very special moment that is so dear to my heart.

Unfortunately, I lost my mother at the tender age of twelve and Travis was nine. This was in July of 1990 on her sister Debra's birthday. She passed over in the morning after waving bye to her little girl. It had only been a year since being diagnosed with cancer. The cancer went from the breast, the lungs and to the brain extremely fast. My mother was only thirty-one when she died.

My father wasn't physically present when my mother passed away and I had to call him on the telephone. It was a critical moment with me losing my mother. I needed to have and wanted to have my father with me at all times. My father was by our side at the funeral. I was on one side of him while Travis was on the other side. I fought back the tears at the funeral. It was one the hardest things I ever experienced and impossible not to cry. I wanted to stay strong for my brother Travis. Our father didn't come to the cemetery for the burial because it was too much for him to handle.

Out of eight children my mother Bonnie was the second youngest of the girls and was the first and only child to die. My mother was loved by all whom knew her. She was absolutely gorgeous, loving, and caring as a mother, daughter, sister and friend.

My mother absolutely adored her children when she was living. Our relationship with her was incredible. She was open and honest with us. It allowed my brother Travis and I to talk about any and everything. I wouldn't have wanted it any other way. This woman possessed her very own style and grace in every aspect.

My mother Bonnie was versatile with both hair and fashion. She loved wearing sterling silver rings and bracelets. Red lipstick was her favorite. My father Gary describes my mother as being drop dead gorgeous. My father knew it and everyone else agreed. I only wish I knew what it was like to grow up with her.

The space between seeing our father was even greater now. It felt like my brother and I had lost both parents in actuality. Every child needs their father and mother in their life. I know within my heart that my father loved us then and he loves us dearly now. However, at that time he chose to live his life in a manner that didn't include his children. I felt like my father did everything possible to show us that he didn't want his family in his life. He could have very well wanted to be with us, but didn't show it.

Overall, he's a great man. I have to say that no matter what, our time spent will always be cherished. I'm happy that he is my father and that I have been blessed to know who my father is. I wouldn't want it any other way.

My father has told me some of the best stories about my mother and the times they shared. Maybe one of his purpose's in my life is to tell me stories of my mother. He reminds me of how wonderful my mother was and how blessed he was to have met her. He respected my mother and loved her to no end.

Anytime that I have shared with my father Gary has been unforgettable. I know the man that I call daddy is without a shadow of a doubt my father. His personality, characteristics, humor, attentiveness and intuition say that I'm his child.

The time with him seems short, but it is priceless. The time has been enough to realize our similarities in one another. It's important to know our parent's because we get a percentage of our personality from them. Life is better when we know our genetics. My father and I were able to see and analyze many things about each other. I'm grateful for the time shared. I will always love my father. I respect his decision on how he chooses to live his life. My father told me that my mother's death affected him tremendously and changed his life forever. I truly believe my father and appreciate him sharing his feelings with me. I would have never known that if it wasn't for our short time spent.

As children we need direction from our parents because they have already lived what we are experiencing. When you don't have either parent to reach out to, you literally feel alone in the world. A scenario like this gives you a different outlook on life. You can make it out here on your own, but it makes it harder. Ultimately, when it's only you. Your parents can't save you from life. Life happens and you have to be prepared for it.

I know in my heart the passing of my mother really affected my father. I don't feel like this is an excuse. Everyone doesn't handle tragedy the same way.

When someone experiences tragedy with the interaction of street drugs, it alters life decisions that are made from day to day.

Over the years I have shown my father that I'm here for him. Even though I didn't feel he was there for me as a child, teenager or an adult. This affected me just as much as losing my mother. I believe that due to the circumstances, I should be the best daughter regardless. I'm okay with any attempt. A simple phone call will put a smile on my face from my daddy.

No matter how I thought about how he should have been there for me, I always wanted to help him out. My father told me and even appeared to want my help financially and with the drugs. I have a big heart and have always enjoyed helping someone if possible. Sometimes I wouldn't have that much money, but I would help him out anyway. I would bend over backwards to help my father and make sure he was okay. Just knowing that without him I wouldn't be here is enough for me to do what I can.

The main thing was his displaying that he wanted to help himself and that would give me initiative. If he ever showed me he wasn't helping himself then I would have to refrain from helping him. My father has five children, two by my mother, and three with three other women. I hoped he would want to change his life at some point so he could be the father that we had all dreamed of. I felt that my siblings and I longed for this more than he did.

Whenever my Grandmother Helen is thinking of my mother and missing her she calls me to come over or just to talk. She always wants me around her because she feels my presence helps her with my mother's absence. I usually go over to my Grandmother Helen's house and lay on her bed with her. That really makes her feel better and she enjoys my company. I enjoy her company. I like to be up under her as well.

My brother Travis and I began living with my Aunt Tama when my mother died in 1990. My Aunt Tama wasn't married and didn't have any children at this time. I told her that my mother Bonnie and I had a talk before she passed away. My mother told me that I could have a boy over at age thirteen. I was looking forward to my thirteenth birthday. It's a special year for most children because you get excited about becoming a teenager. My mother had given me an even bigger reason to look forward to my big day. However, my mother died two months earlier before my big day.

I told my Aunt Tama what my mother had promised me. There was no proof. It was hard for her to believe, but she did. I was even given a thirteenth birthday party that lasted until midnight. I think it was to take my mind off everything that had taken place with my mother. All of my friends from school and my neighborhood were invited. We lived in Woodmere Park off of Phillips Avenue on Rayston Drive. It's within walking distance of Claremont. The party lasted until midnight and the last song that played was "Make It Last Forever" by Keith Sweat. It was the summer of 1990. Our house was on the corner, the streets were packed after the party was over. We didn't want the party to end.

My Aunt Tama always wanted to make me happy, as well as my brother Travis. My brother Travis was dealing with his own outcry for attention. My brother went to stay with our Grandmother Helen at the age of 14. Travis begin drinking and smoking weed to ease the pain of our mother's loss. Travis attended Dudley, but eventually was sent to a military school.

Aunt Tama would do anything that she could for me and Travis. We still felt incomplete. No one had anything to do with our emptiness, but at some point I thought they did. I felt that someone owed me and my brother something. Then, I could only concentrate on the void coming from the woman who had given birth to me. That was giving me a feeling of extreme loneliness.

Overall, throughout life I felt as though it was me against the world— literally. Everyone is on their own and don't realize it until adversity presents itself. I had no mother. My living father had chosen to spend his time away from his family and on drugs. When I was going to Dudley High School my best friend Val introduced me to a guy.

We went to Winston-Salem, NC to meet him. This is where he lived at the time with his mother. Once meeting him, we hit it off right away and started talking on the phone until late in the morning. I had no idea that he would become one of my best friends and we would have a unique relationship. Brad seemed to be just what I needed in my life at this time.

Brad

While going through life without parental guidance. I felt alone and ended up meeting someone. I met Brad when I was 15 years old. Brad came along unexpectedly and we could talk about anything. He had his own style when it came to dressing. Brad wore Nautica shirts, Khaki pants and Polo boots. He liked shopping at Eddie Bauer and Stein Mart. I didn't shop at either place until meeting him. Brad was five-foot-seven, brown skin, full lips, and kept his hair cut close which showed off his wave pattern. I liked him because he was cute in his own way and the average female wouldn't even take notice to him. It was just something about him. He had a wonderful sense of humor and could make anyone laugh. I liked that in a guy and found it attractive. Brad was known for cracking jokes in school. Most of all, he didn't judge me and I didn't judge him. I appreciated that more than anything.

This was the first time that I was able to express myself about the way I felt after my mother had died. Once my mother died, I didn't believe in God anymore. I lost all hope of the existence of the higher power. I didn't feel that my mother should have been taken away from me or anyone else that loved her. I was going through the grieving process. My feelings had been buried deep in my soul. I was able to express the pain and hurt from the absence of both parents. He didn't mind wiping away my tears. I needed this in my life. We became true friends and formed a true bond that would last a lifetime. We had a special type of closeness and it was as if we understood one another. I found out that we were similar because we both needed someone to talk to. Brad and my brother Travis began to form their own bond. They would hang together from time to time.

We became a shoulder to lean on for one another during life's trials and tribulations. Even through the love from him and my family, I was still struggling with pain on the inside that needed to be healed. No one else would be able to make me feel better and I had to do it on my own. I had no idea that I had to fix myself and was looking to others to help me. I had to get over this false reality of what I thought my life should have been like.

We started dating at the age of 16. Brad ended up becoming my high school sweetheart. I had Brad and begin to open up about myself. I opened up to him because I knew that he really cared about me. I felt safe with him and like he wouldn't let anything happen to me. He would do anything for me as well.

We were like most teenagers and would go on double dates, dress alike, and take pictures together. I never would have imagined this man ever doing anything to hurt me. We went out from the end of 9th grade until our senior year in high school. We were both in the same grade.

Brad went to Smith High School and I went to Dudley High School. I didn't go to my high school prom, but I went with Brad to his high school prom during our junior year. Brad drove us to the prom in his father's BMW. It was grey, two doors, with a sunroof, and sporty. We met the other teenage couples at Darryl's on High Point Road for dinner. My Aunt Tama had given me permission to stay out all night if I wanted. Besides she was comfortable with the fact that Brad and I was a couple. My Aunt Tama talked about the birds and the bees with me when I was of age. I stayed out until 2 a.m. on prom night, but not all night. Brad had spent all his money on the clothes and dinner; therefore, we couldn't get a hotel room like some of the other teenagers. Neither one of us went to the prom, during our 12th grade year. We were okay with that because we experienced all the joys of prom from the previous year as juniors.

We were both dealing with things at home even though we were only teenagers. Brad stayed with his father, step-mother and step-brother. We found comfort in one another and things grew from there. I lived with my Aunt Tama, so we both had broken homes. During my high school years, I continued to be rebellious and didn't want to listen to anyone. I didn't want to listen to anyone if it wasn't my mother. I didn't care if the person was right or wrong. I was angry because of my mother's absence and at certain times it really showed. The only thing that mattered to me was that I wanted my mother. I only wanted to be disciplined by her and no one else.

At moments, I thought that I was out of place as a teenager because neither of my parents was there for me. The people around me would ask me questions like, where is your mom or who do you live with. It made me feel out of place amongst my peers. It always bothered me, but I wouldn't let it show. I covered my pain and suffering on the inside. I appeared happy because I would always be smiling and never told anyone.

I had opened up to Brad. It wasn't enough to clear the pain I had been holding in my heart. I felt overwhelmed with my emotions and everyday life at this point. I thought that suicide was the best answer. I looked in the medicine cabinet one night and my mind reacted without a second thought. I grabbed different bottles of pills that were not even for me. I began taking one pill at a time that was prescribed for who knows what.

At that very moment I had no idea of the severity of my actions. I didn't think twice about hurting myself or the people in my life. This was my cry for help. I wasn't sure of the type of help needed. When someone overdoses they don't realize that they don't die instantly. It's slow and agonizing.

I lost count of the amount of pills that I had consumed. Afterwards, I called my boyfriend about my thoughtless decision. I wanted someone to know about my attempt. My Aunt Tama was in the other room the entire time and had no idea what was going on. Brad's mother worked at a hospital in Winston-Salem. He knew that she would give useful information because of her background in the medical field. She told him that he needed to get me to the hospital immediately. Brad relayed the message to me and told me that he was on his way.

In the meantime, I'm at home feeling miserable with side effects like nausea and dizziness. Jeopardizing my life was one of the most irrational things that I could have chosen to do. I was in my bedroom waiting on my boyfriend and I was getting sleepier and sleepier by the minute. His mother had already warned me not to fall asleep. Brad finally arrived at 8 p.m. and rushed me to the hospital. I told my aunt that I would be back.

The staff immediately put me in a room in the emergency department under the circumstances. They were moving fast due to my life-threatening condition. I sat on the side of the hospital bed and was given a medical concoction as a remedy. I was instructed to drink the entire mixture and told this would make me vomit. Once, the solution got into my system, I began to vomit profusely. I vomited until all of the pills were out of my system and off of my stomach. You can only imagine how good I felt after vomiting.

It was 11:30 p.m. and I needed to call and let my Aunt Tama know of my stupidity, now that I was going to be okay. She wanted to know if she needed to come to the hospital. I reassured her that she didn't. I told her that I was with Brad and he was about to bring me home. I also let her know that if it wasn't for Brad reacting in a timely manner then who knows what the outcome would have been.

When I got home I rested. The next day my Aunt Tama talked with me. I had to tell her the reason I made such a foolish decision. I told her that I missed my mother so much. I had let it get the best of me. I had love, but didn't feel it. I told her life just seemed so unfair to me and that I felt like I was being punished. She consoled me by hugging and kissing me. She told me that she understood what I was going through, but if I ever felt that way again to come and talk to her. She thanked Brad for getting me to the hospital and taking care of me. The rush to the hospital due to an overdose was enough. I didn't want to experience that ever again. I realized how much I wanted to live and how selfish my actions were.

My boyfriend and I both received cars at the age of 16. Brad drove a light blue Nissan Sentra, four doors, tinted windows, chrome rims and a booming system. He often played Regulators by Warren G in his car. The front of his car read "Chronic Zone" across the top of the front window. I drove a regular white two door Nissan Sentra with "2 Cute" on the front bumper with no boom. The sign that read "2 Cute" was my auntie's idea. Brad had a car system and I wanted one, so he put one in my car. I would listen to "So Funkdafied" by the artist called Da Brat in my car. The bass in this song really hit hard. I always thought it was cute that we drove the same vehicles. I never knew the reason he wanted to announce "Chronic Zone" to everyone. It really didn't matter to me because I liked him. Brad wasn't selling drugs when we first met, but we would smoke marijuana together.

As time went on, I still didn't want to listen to my Aunt Tama or anyone else concerning my actions. I was stubborn as a mule and wanted to rebel. I wanted to make my own choices that ultimately were poor. Brad had been going through things at home for a while and eventually was kicked out of the house. This house was shared by his father, step-mother and step-brother. We would be together for the majority of the day and majority of time during the night. Brad took me to work at McDonald's and picked me up most nights.

When he moved out it was to a house in a nice neighborhood and he rented the top portion of the home. It was the end of our senior year when this transition took place. This was the same neighborhood that we had hung out in during our teenage years. My best friend Val whom introduced me to Brad lived down the street from Brad's new home. Brad's place was a two level house and the people that lived there didn't use the upstairs. The upstairs included two rooms and a full bathroom.

Brad had been working since I had known him, but things were about to change. Brad was paying rent and would need more income. Brad started hustling to make more money. I thought about my environment, but none of it mattered. The only thing that mattered was that I felt like Brad was the only person I could count on. Even though that wasn't the case. He understood me and I needed that. We already knew so much about one another. I continued to have issues at home or make them worse than they were. There were no real problems at home with my Aunt Tama.

I wanted to be rebellious. I didn't want anyone telling me what to do. I was angry simply because I no longer had my loving mother. This resulted in me leaving my perfectly comfortable environment to live in a "crack house" just to be with my boyfriend. The couple that owned this home smoked cigarettes to no end and did drugs.

I moved in with Brad even though my aunt was against it. I insisted on leaving and soon moved my clothes into the new place. I bought new sheets for the bed, cleaned the rooms and bathroom. I decorated the bathroom to my liking. I was officially out on my own at the age of 17. Thinking and acting like I was grown.

My aunt would always tease me while growing up and say that I was a woman. She would check on me, say she missed me and that she wanted me to come home. I didn't want to at that time, but I didn't realize that it would change soon. It felt good not to have anyone over you necessarily. I was worried about the illegal activity, but continued to stay there with Brad. If I went back home, I would have to leave him. I didn't want to do that.

Finally, my Aunt Tama and I came to an agreement. I asked if Brad could come back with me and she agreed to it. He would have to pay rent though. My aunt agreed because we had already been living together, but she was cool with it. I couldn't believe that she actually said "yes"! Brad went from renting the upstairs of a home to paying rent to my aunt.

I should have finished high school in 1995. I was too busy doing the things that I shouldn't have been doing. I chose to skip school doing things that weren't in my best interest. I had other friends that skipped, but they passed and were able to graduate in 1995.

I met Lola while attending Dudley and we became friends. Lola was five-foot-seven with a light complexion and long hair. Lola and I were both in the same situation. I wasn't driving at the time. Lola would come to get me in her cream Nissan 240sx. We had to attend Guilford Technical Community College's Adult Program in Greensboro during the summer. We were in school while the teens that followed the rules were enjoying their summer. Lola and I received our diplomas in August of 1996 from Guilford Technical Community College Adult Program. We were determined to get our diplomas no matter what it took. My brother Travis graduated from North Carolina Tarheel Challenge in Clinton, NC during the summer of 1997. Layla graduated from Page High School in Greensboro in 1998.

Betrayal

Throughout high school Brad and I associated with the same people. I attended Dudley High School from 1991 until 1995. Brad was at Smith. His boys were talking to my girls and we would all hang out. One particular guy named Vic stayed with his brother Nazeer. Nazeer was light skinned with freckles across the nose and under the eyes. He had a nice grade of hair and had a style about him. They were close in age. They were no more than eight years apart. Vic could pretty much do whatever he wanted. It was as though he had his own place. Well,

Vic did since there was no parental advisory.

Everyone would gather at Vic's house since his brother didn't mind. Vic would have music, drinking and smoking. Brad was over there all of the time and I knew that girls were usually there as well. Vic was a ladies' man. Vic was a light complexion of brown with a greenish, brown mixture to his eyes. He had that up north swag about him that attracted the ladies even more. There was nothing I could say about it because that was his boy. It had been going on for a while now.

We continued to go together until we finally reached a turning point in our relationship. We began to grow apart and needed time away from each other. Brad ended up moving out of my aunt's house, but we remained very close friends. We continued doing things that couples do. We just needed some time apart since being together most of our high school years. Together we experienced more than the average teenager. It was time that we both experience life apart.

When we broke up, he was hustling harder in the streets. The entire time I had no idea on what level he was doing things on. We always kept in touch, but never went into detail about his street life. I really didn't want to know about it. Some things are better off that way. I wouldn't have believed it anyway because I didn't see him in that way. His character didn't show street credibility.

During this time, we were about 18 years old. Brad was going out with other girls and I was seeing other guys. I was bothered by the break up because I still had feelings for him. One reason we both had feelings for each other was the mere fact that we were still being intimate. There was no need of me worrying about what he was doing now, but I did. I always knew that there were females over there and what was possibly taking place.

Val introduced me to Brad and she was still hanging out over at Vic's. Val had a friend name Camille that was going out with Brad's friend. Val was light skinned with curves, attractive and had long hair. Camille was pretty too.

One night Brad, my ex-boyfriend at this time, said he had something to tell me. What he wanted to tell me would change my view on life and trust. Brad told me that something happened one of the nights he was hanging over Vic's house. Of course, females were always there with them. I already knew what went on over at Vic's. I had to brace myself because I could tell this wasn't sounding like the best of news. Brad told me that Val was there this particular night. They all played a game that required each person to take their clothes off. One of those games where if you get the answer wrong you have to strip.

Overall, one thing led to another and Brad told me that he had been with

Val. I was never sure about what exactly happened between them, but I knew that they had a form of intimacy. It was something that I didn't want to envision. I listened to his side of the story and then to Val's side. The information was devastating and I didn't know how to react. I was distraught and felt confused about the position that either of them would play in my life. I cried for several days. It was as though someone had died.

Two of my closest friends had betrayed me and I felt like I had been played. I wasn't sure if either deserved to be in my life at this point. I wanted to cut them both off and tell them to be together. I had in my mind that I would never be able to trust Val around any other boyfriend in my future. Brad was the first one to tell me about the two of them messing around. It made me appreciate him for beating Val to the punch. I weighed my thoughts and decided to continue dealing with Brad.

I loved both of them dearly, but would never trust them in my presence at the same time. My mind would always wonder what they were feeling or thinking about each other. For my peace of mind, I couldn't have Val around us anymore. She jeopardized our friendship over lust. She shouldn't have introduced me to Brad if she wanted him. Maybe Val didn't want Brad and the situation only made me feel this way. Val was dating Brad's stepbrother Grayland. Everyone involved seemed to be over it and moving on with their lives. Val always said guys come and go. She was definitely right and I agreed with her. Val wanted me to get over it, but I couldn't get past this particular situation. Regardless, I still loved Val and she loved me. Things would never be the same between any of us. The pack had been broken.

I lived at home for about two years after high school and then moved out on my own. I was able to rent my first apartment when I was 20. I was the first one to get a place after high school. The apartment was a two bedroom with one bathroom. It was cozy and cute, just for me, on the East side of town. I lived on Phillips Avenue at New Garden Place

Apartments across from the top hill store. The store was literally at the top of the hill on Phillip's Avenue. That's how the name of the store came about.

My Aunt Tama helped me get the apartment and she made sure it was fully furnished. My aunt had recently had her daughter Kiana and we had already discussed me being a full-time baby sitter. This way she wouldn't have to place her child with strangers in a daycare. It was cool with me because I didn't have to leave the house after a long night.

My house quickly became the hangout and I loved it. We stayed up late drinking, smoking and playing cards. The music stayed pumping on my 60-CD disc changer. Songs by Jay-Z, Notorious Big,

Nas and Lil' Kim played just to name a few. We had some serious parties that led to people staying the night. My friends and cousins would bring their guy friends over. I didn't mind because we were having fun and there was enough room.

I was babysitting my cousin Kiana, so I decided I wanted to do hair. I kept Kiana until she was 2 years old. Then she went to daycare. I was getting paid $150 a week. I began doing hair at 15 years old. I figured that I might as well get paid for it. I enrolled at Leon's Beauty School. The same cosmetology school that my mother Bonnie attended. You couldn't tell me I wasn't on my way. I wanted to own a salon with the hopes of completing my mother's dream. I wanted to follow in her foot steps.

I started Leon's Beauty School and met an African man named Za. I met Za at the Raleigh Street Pool Room in June of 1999. He stood about five-foot-six with a dark complexion and a low haircut. Za was in his mid-thirties. He looked older in the face. Za had tribal markings on his forehead. His left and right cheek were marked also. Za's tribal markings were extreme, but I knew that this was part of the African culture. People are marked to know what tribe they belong to. They appeared to be scars. They were embedded deeply into his skin and very obvious to the eye. A person in their right mind would have quickly gone in the opposite direction.

Regardless of the markings on his face, I wanted to hang out with him. Za wanted to take care of me and purchase things for me. Za wanted to make me his wife. I told him that I didn't want to be in a relationship. I often met my best friend Deon at Raleigh Street Pool Room. Deon was five-foot-eleven, dark chocolate complexion with a very close fade. Deon was 24 years old. We were children when we first met. We both lived in Claremont. Over time I became like a sister to Deon. We have real love for each other. We would hang out there throughout the week and on the weekends. Deon and I were always out and about. People often thought we were dating, but were only thick as thieves. Our relationship is monogamous. The pool room was a popular meeting spot to most people that enjoyed a good game of pool.

It was the summer of 1999. Za was at Raleigh Street Pool Room and we exchanged numbers. Za began showering me with drugs and money from the moment we met. On the very same day of meeting. The things that Za offered me made me want to hang out with him. I rode with Za that first night to get some marijuana. Za may have been selling it, but I had no idea. I felt that Za thought he could make me do things with him because he had money. I left the pool room and went to the McDonald's on

Summit Avenue only to find him there as well.

Za began following me and I didn't realize it. We had been intimate a few times, but not enough for feelings to form. I would visit him at his home on North Elm Eugene Street. He would prepare food at his place. We didn't go out to eat or to the movies. I visited Za's house frequently over the course of the month. It had been a little over a month since meeting Za and I had to cut him off.

Soon, he was following me around town and watching me. Za had more than one car and would be in a different car each time. Za lived in the same apartment complex as my cousin Venus. Venus's house was in walking distance. I never told Za about my cousin living there. One night I went to put a relaxer in Venus's hair and I could feel someone staring through the window. I had a strange feeling about Za's actions from that night forward. This was the first time that I had encountered a real life stalker. I had just left Venus's house. I was talking to my cousin Los' in front of Red's on Church Street and Za seen me. Los' was leaning over inside the passenger side window and talking to me. I noticed that he was behind me in his car, but didn't speak to me. Za was hoping I didn't notice him.

Later that night, Za told me that I was cheating on him and having sex with other guys. Za assumed and didn't bother to ask me. The money, drugs and cars that

Za offered sounded good. Just not from him. I never told Za that I was his girlfriend or that he was my boyfriend. I didn't want to make a commitment. I wanted to talk and be with anyone I chose without any restrictions.

I began thinking a restraining order was needed to keep him away from me. That wasn't enough. Za began to threaten my livelihood. He would ride through my parking lot day and night. Pagers also known as beepers were popular in 1999. I still had one. Za would page me with the numbers 666. This made me think about the devil. The pages from Za never stopped. Za would page me saying "go to hell!" Other times he would say that he loved me. It would scare the hell out of me! Za was insane! He was the devil in disguise. I had to tell my family what was going on.

One day I was out cruising near Ray Warren projects and Za spotted me. He pulled his car right in front of mine and blocked me. He ran over to my car and pulled a gun on me. Za fired it in the air as if he was warning me. I didn't know what to expect or what he would do next. He was capable of doing anything to me after what I had just witnessed. I immediately sped off. I drove over the median on Lee Street away from Ray Warren projects in Greensboro.

The police could have tried to stop me and I would have continued with no thoughts of a ticket. I called my closest family and friends to let them know about Za's behavior. I was terrified that he was going to catch up to me. I drove out of sight as fast as I could.

My Uncle Butch decided I needed a gun. He told me to go purchase a gun permit. I took a warrant out on Za. Afterwards, I applied for the gun permit. My record was clean at this time, so I knew it wouldn't be an issue. Then my Uncle Butch purchased me a gun. It was a chrome, baby 380 with a black grip. The 380 was registered in my name. My Uncle Butch wanted me to keep it with me at all times. I was nervous about having a gun at first. I had never even shot one before. I drove with the 380 on the passenger seat at all times unless someone was riding with me. The gun couldn't be concealed.

My best friend Deon decided to stay in my presence more than the usual due to the chaos. Deon didn't want me to stay at home alone. I didn't want to be alone. Deon brought a gun over every time he came over. Many nights Deon spent the night with me. I really appreciated him because I hadn't been getting any good sleep at night. The police agreed with the measures we had taken, otherwise they suggested that I go into protective custody. This type of home provides a safe dwelling for a victim out of harms way and away from the suspect. The police asked me more than once about this option. They also suggested me going to stay with family out of town until this blew over. My family and friends were aware, but I chose to do it another way. I thought about staying with my Aunt Tama at her home in the country. I decided to stay close to home and not run. My family and friends had me in their prayers doing this ordeal.

My life was different now. I only wanted close family and friends around me. I already had trust issues and this was the icing on the cake. I didn't know who associated with Za or even who Za could have paid to watch me. Deon, my cousin Nya and I were at McDonald's on Summit Avenue in the drive-thru. This was a couple of days after the incident on Lee Street. A gunshot was fired towards my

Nissan Sentra. The gunshot that was fired struck the hood of my car. I had no idea it was a bullet. I thought someone was playing around and a baseball hit the car. We pulled out of the drive-thru then pulled to the side of the restaurant to check the car out.

We stepped out of the car and walked around the car to examine it. There was a bullet hole in the hood of my car. The bullet hole was at the top of the hood and underneath the front window. There was no doubt that the bullet was pointed in my direction. I was shaken up tremendously after this life-threatening episode. I was afraid that the person was still looking on and ready to fire. This was the first time I ever felt someone was trying to kill me and had no idea why.

Deon and I drove to my Uncle Butch's house to let Nya out. I was able to talk to my uncle face to face and he could see my frustration. I was afraid of what Za could be planning. My uncles on my mother's side were fed up with Za messing with me. They wanted to see just who was bothering their niece. I called Za and within minutes he was circling my apartment complex.

Whenever I knew that Za was close to my home, I would begin reading my bible. I would read scripture after scripture until Za left my premises. This is where I knew to go for strength and hope that this too shall pass along with prayer.

My favorite scriptures are in the Book Of Psalms. The apartment complex was shaped in a horseshoe. You entered on one side and circled around to exit onto Phillips Avenue. It was one of those places that was one way in and one way out. This is the worst type of layout. There were three apartment buildings and each building had parking spaces in front of them.

My uncles posted up everywhere with their weapons. They decided not to be in front of my place. My uncles were at the corner of the apartment building hidden by the bushes. The purpose was to be in a position and not to bring attention to my apartment. They wanted to show Za how it felt to be watched. Therefore, Za wouldn't suspect that anyone was watching his every move. This was definitely a scene out of a movie.

Each of my three uncles had shotguns and was willing to take Za out if he didn't stop harassing me. My uncles were so upset about my involvement with such a crazy ass person. They wanted to know where I had met him and what made me get involved with him. I had no idea, but it was on the list of poor choices for me. I was more disappointed in myself for being vulnerable with the devil. That night Za circled the parking lot to my complex. Za left abruptly after I called to let him know that he was being watched.

A few hours later, I received a call from the Greensboro Police Department.

Za had been pulled over for some issues with his vehicle. Once, he was pulled over, the police ran his name and noticed the warrant for his arrest. Za was apprehended and taken into custody.

The police told me when they opened Za's trunk they found dead chickens. What in the world was he into? Voodoo maybe. I had no idea. He was into something crazy, or about to do something that I didn't want to be part of. Za was arrested in September of 1999. I was so thankful that Za was in custody now. I could try and rest. It had been a total nightmare the past few weeks while feeling that my life was in jeopardy. I hadn't been able to sleep.

Everyone around me had been deprived of their life for trying to make sure I was okay. Everyone was relieved, but it still wasn't over. Now that he was in custody, he would have to appear in court. The police wanted me and two other females to testify against him.

Brad and I were still keeping in touch. I didn't want to talk to anyone new after my previous situation. I felt like I couldn't trust anyone. Brad always reminded me that he wanted us to get back together, but I didn't want to. I knew that he was still doing his thing and getting money in the streets.

One day I went to visit Brad at a new place that he had gotten. It was an area that I would have wanted to live in.

The place was very nice and in a prominent community known as Adams Farm in Greensboro. I knew Brad was making good money by the looks of his place. I never knew what level of getting money he was on. I just knew he was doing his thing. The home ran him about a $1,000 a month. Brad had bolts on all the bedroom doors and that bothered me. Brad didn't have to worry about me ever staying over because of that. I didn't ask any questions, but it made me think that something serious was going on in his life. I didn't want any parts of it either.

I knew this would be my first and last visit to his apartment no matter what. I wasn't feeling the set up. He could visit me, but I shouldn't have allowed that from the looks of his place. We would see one another every now and then. It wasn't on a regular basis anymore. We talked on the phone more than we visited one another. The love was never lost between us. We were at different places in our lives. We were both okay with that. Brad's schedule was busy and he was seeing a female. It could have been more than one. I didn't know and it didn't matter to me. We were always friends first.

Brad stayed in the apartment for about a year and then moved to a house. The home was in a middle class neighborhood near Southmont that had been around since I was younger. I lived in Southmont when I first met Brad. My brother Travis and I lived there with our

Aunt Tama. It was a community off of Randleman Road in Greensboro. He even asked me to move in with him, but I told him that I didn't want to. I hadn't went back to cosmetology school, but that was the plan. I was stilling doing hair on the side. Brad knew of my plan and talked about an idea with me. His new place had a room in the back and he asked me if I wanted to turn it into a salon. He kept on insisting it was a good idea. It would have been a great idea if the environment was right.

Something about his lifestyle kept me away from getting as close as we were in high school. Brad was driving a new car and eventually he had two new cars. I thought he was doing well for himself and

I was happy for him. Brad's brother was still living with him from back when I lived with Brad.

Soon, where Brad lived was no longer a place he wanted to stay. Brad wanted to get away from Greensboro. He would tell me that he had people in Atlanta and he really wanted to move down there. Brad asked me if I would move with him a few times. My feelings for Brad were still strong, but in the back of my mind something wasn't adding up with the way he was living.

I still had my own place on Phillips Avenue. Brad and I lived our separate lives. We would bump and grind from time to time. One night, Brad came over to spend the night with me. It was a quiet night and we were there alone. It wasn't normal for no one to be at my house. We talked; listened to the "My Life" cd by Mary J. Blige, smoked marijuana and was intimate.

Brad and I went to bed, but I couldn't sleep because of his snoring. This was something new to me because Brad didn't snore when we first met. Even if he was tired, he didn't snore. I thought this was strange. I kept nudging him and telling him that he was snoring with hopes that it would stop.

It was the late part of September and there was no need for the air condition. The weather was nice and comfortable outside. I had the windows open in both bedrooms. I couldn't sleep. I was lying in bed next to Brad. My mind started to wonder about this and that. It felt so good that night because the wind was blowing extremely hard. There was a breeze like no other coming through the windows. I was in bed watching the trees blow up and down, then side to side outside of the windows. I had never seen the wind blow as hard as it did that night. I didn't have the television on, so it was just peace and quiet.

The wind picked up so much that it frightened me. I wanted to wake Brad up, but I didn't. I was hoping that it would wake him, but he heard absolutely nothing. Brad was knocked out. The wind blew so hard it knocked the artificial tree down in the other bedroom. I immediately jumped out of bed to make sure it was only the wind. The wind felt great, but I was scared as hell at the force. It felt like a tornado was sweeping through the apartment. The magnitude of the wind was unforgettable. It felt like something literally swept through my apartment that night and took us with it. Brad left that next morning and we didn't see each other for weeks.

A couple of months after that, I received a phone call. My cousin Layla used to talk on the phone to one of Brad's friends. They didn't talk anymore, but he still had her number. Keith called with some really bad news. Immediately following Keith's call, my cousin Layla called to bare the news to me.

I couldn't believe what I was hearing. I didn't want to believe it. Brad had been shot on the street where he lived. Brad was leaving his home to run errands. He pulled out of his driveway and then proceeded to the end of the street. Brad came to a complete stop at the stop sign and someone shot him. I couldn't understand how someone could be so cruel to someone. I wanted to know what Brad had done to make someone this angry. I tried to get myself together in hopes of finding out what had happened.

Brad was a person that I cared for and loved. I began calling everywhere hoping to get anyone to give me details. I called Moses Cone Hospital and they couldn't give me any information. I wanted to know if it was true before I over reacted. I was frantic at this point and I was unable to drive. There was no way that I could drive in this state of mind.

I was scared, nervous, and confused about the circumstances. I was shaking uncontrollably with horrible thoughts of the worst possible news. I only wanted to talk to Brad and hear his voice. I needed to know that he was okay.

My friend Lola came to drive me around. First, I rode by his house and it was pitch black. No sign of anyone being there. I didn't get a good vibe looking towards his home. We had the music low as we traveled from place to place. Lola could feel my pain. Second, I rode to the hospital. However, no information can be given on gunshot victims. It's considered private information. Third, I contacted his mother and father to find out if anything really happened. I wasn't getting anywhere.

Unfortunately, Brad died that night from a gunshot wound. Brad was 23 years old. He was shot on the right side of the body where the major organs in the lower abdomen are located. I was devastated by the news and my life felt as though it had been crumbled into a thousand pieces. A part of me left with him and I felt empty once again. Brad was someone that I could confide in and he knew everything about me. I didn't keep anything from him. I would have never imagined him being into the streets so deep that it would result in him being killed. I was afraid because of my association with Brad. I had no idea what this was about. I wasn't over the traumatic state involving Za and now this.

My brother Travis had spent the night with Brad the night before his death. Brad took Travis home the morning of the incident. Brad was actually on his way back to pick Travis up before the incident happened. Brad had planned to pick up Travis by 2:30 pm after going by the cleaners. He was murdered around 2:00 pm that afternoon. It was the weekend of A&T State University's Homecoming in October of 1999.

The investigators were questioning anyone associated with Brad or who had contact with him. The police department was investigating the case as a homicide. The Greensboro Police Department probably had his phone as the resource for contacting anyone listed in the phone. The investigator called me to set up an appointment and interrogate me. I was treated as if I was the one that shot him. I never even made it to the hospital to see him before he died.

The police were on a mission to get the killer or any information no matter what it took. They showed me pictures of Brad in the hospital fighting for his life. Brad was hooked up to IV tubes, monitors and oxygen. His eyes were closed as he lay there in the hospital bed. The pictures were absolutely grueling to the eyes of anyone that cared for this man. I thought it was a horrible way to try and get information out of me. I knew they were doing their job, but how low could they go. I cried and cried after viewing the photos. I had to endure the cruelty imposed on me that day. I had no clue what happened and obviously neither did they. I had more long nights that involved nightmares. I finally tried to get some rest.

I was back to feeling as if I was all alone in this world. The guy with whom I shared my deepest secrets had been taken away from me. It wasn't just me. Brad had a family that loved and cared for him. I had lost my mother, Brad, and my dad wasn't present in my life at this time. I was barely 22 years of age and so much was going on in the world with no guidance. At a time when I needed someone that knew me inside and out. More and more it seemed like it was me against the world. The funeral was in his hometown of Winston-Salem. It had been about a week and I was still in no condition to drive. My Aunt Jean decided to drive me and my brother Travis to the funeral. We waited on my cousin Pooh, but she never showed. This had us late for his funeral. The funeral was in Winston-Salem, NC. It wasn't a short drive either.

Upon my arrival, the funeral had already started and the eulogy was taking place. Brad's funeral was packed to capacity with family and friends from high school. The casket was already closed. I walked to the front where the family was seated. I was looking for Brad's mother because I wanted to ask her something. I wanted to know if she would open the casket back up. She refused. I only wanted to see him one last time and that seemed to be too much to ask for. I was more upset with myself rather than his mother. I knew it had to be hard on her and even harder to open the casket once more. I started to tell myself that Brad didn't want me to see him in that condition. I had to truly convince myself that Brad wanted it this way just to keep my sanity. I thought I was going to lose it.

My view towards love changed again. I experienced a love loss with my mother and a man early on in life. They were totally different, but both broke my heart. Honestly, I wanted someone to blame, but ultimately had no one. This made me realize that death is a part of life whether I like it or not.

Brad came from a good family. I really didn't understand his lifestyle. Brad had a thrill for the streets and the fast money. Brad didn't have to hustle. I was young. Way too young to understand what it meant to hustle! I was learning fast. Brad's father worked for RJ Reynolds and his mother worked for Baptist Hospital in Winston-Salem, NC. Brad's mother and I have remained friends. We keep in touch during the year and especially around the holidays.

I felt as though I didn't want to ever be in a relationship again. I didn't want to love again. My thoughts were if I kept love out of the equation, I would be okay. My hopes were that this way of thinking would prepare me for the future. It wouldn't hurt as bad whenever I lost again. This would be one of the hardest things to do. We have no control over who we love or when we love. I knew deep in my heart that nothing lasts forever. People are designed to leave at some point.

After Brad's death I was afraid to love anyone. I had a bittersweet taste about life in general, but giving up wasn't an option for me. On the other hand, I gained strength through each circumstance that I had surpassed. I had gained an unspoken amount of strength and courage.

Afterwards, I put a wall up, so that I wouldn't allow anyone to get close to me. Any existing relationship was okay with me. I didn't want a new one. This was to protect myself from ever being hurt. I didn't realize it was the impossible. I'm such a loving person that this was going to be hard. I wouldn't be able to go through life and not love anyone. It would be difficult going through life and not loving a single soul. I played tough and carried an "I don't care attitude" towards life and anyone who wanted to get close to me for quite a while. I was ready to embrace a change when it came my way.

It was time for Za's trial. It was in February of 2000. I was afraid to take the stand. I hadn't been in a situation like this. I wanted everything to be over. I was willing to do whatever it took. After Za's arrest I found out that he had previously stalked two other females.

Each one of us was present on the day of the trial. We met for the first time at the courthouse and exchanged horror stories. The three of us talked about our relationship with Za and the different actions he had taken against us. One of the females said he fired into her home. The other female was followed around town. It was up to us to prevent Za from actually harming anyone. Za didn't seem to care about anyone's well being. We all wanted the same result in the end. We wanted him far away from us. The three of us took the stand one by one and the judge reached his verdict. The judge ruled that Za had to be deported. This meant that he would return to Africa without ever being able to return to the United States. Whew! I now felt like I could live again.

Finally, I didn't have to think about my every move being monitored or my life being threatened. Even though Za was deported, it took a while before the nightmares ended. It seemed as though every night I was haunted by Za in my dreams. I could see his face each time I closed my eyes. My frame of mind had to heal from the traumatic stress of that escapade. I vowed that I wouldn't ever deal with another African after this experience. I wanted time to myself once this ordeal was behind me. Not involving my family sooner was a poor choice!

Stan

My next relationship came about two years after Brad died. I was 24 years old. We met through mutual friends. My cousins and I were invited to swim at an apartment complex where Stan lived. The apartment was near the airport in Greensboro on Old Oak Ridge Road. Stan was the roommate to Liam whom invited us over. Layla loved to swim. She's an Aquarius and that alone screams water.

Liam went to Smith High School with Val and the other people I had associated with during high school. It was something fun and exciting because I had several females with me and Liam had several guys at his place. Liam had arranged everything. All we had to do was show up. Liam planned to have a pool party which included food, guys, drinking and smoking weed. We listened to 2 Pac's hit "Gangsta Party" and this was definitely our type of party. We had a ball at the swimming pool hanging out with them. This was the start of my relationship with Stan.

Stan had a caramel complexion with dark curly hair and stood about five-foot-eight. He was 26 years old. Stan didn't exercise at all and had a bit of a tummy. He could almost go for a Latino and dressed in a casual manner with Khaki pants and button down shirts. This was around the time that I was thinking about moving.

When I first saw them, I knew that I wanted to live there. I was currently living on Phillips Avenue. The house I lived in during high school was right across the street from the new property that was being built. The new property was Willow Ridge Apartments on Willow Road. It was in walking distance from the house I lived in with my Aunt Tama while attending Dudley High School.

I looked on for months as the builders brought the apartment complex to life. The property that was being built was going to have a swimming pool and a park. It had a clubhouse that could be utilized by the tenants. There would be about seven buildings that would house sixteen people in each. My Aunt Tama looked forward to bringing her daughter Kiana over to swim there. My Aunt Tama talked as though I was already living in the apartment. My aunt suggested that I put in an application and I did. She was pretty sure that I would get it. I was approved and it wasn't long before I could move in.

I really loved this apartment! The property was brand new. I was lucky enough to get one. I remember being so excited when I found out that I was accepted as a tenant. I would be the first to move in. My Aunt Tama was just as excited about my close move. The apartment had two bedrooms, two full baths, and a kitchen bar. It also had a laundry room with a washer and dryer connection along with a dining room. Every tenant had a choice of either tan or hunter green carpet. I chose the hunter green. It would go well with my cream colored sofa, coffee table and kitchen table. The master bedroom had a walk-in closet and a garden tub. The second bedroom had a walk-in closet, but it was half the size of the one in the master bedroom. It did have more shelving and was perfect for storage. It was convenient for family and friends to stay due to the extra space. I was accustomed to having two bedrooms where ever I lived. I enjoyed living alone, but loved to have overnight company. Lola and my other friends would stay with me from time to time. It was cool!

The next time I ran into Stan was during the weekend of A&T State University's homecoming in 2001. We exchanged numbers and kept in contact more often this time. Stan didn't live in Greensboro anymore and was only visiting for the homecoming weekend. He actually lived a couple of cities away in Lexington, NC known as "Lex Vegas" to the surrounding areas. After talking on the phone for a while, we began to see one another in person. Later, he began staying the night with me. He wanted to be with me more and we discussed living together.

I thought he was attractive, funny and a family guy. In the beginning it seemed as though we were a perfect match. When we were getting to know one another it was nice and simple. Stan had two children that lived in his hometown. I was okay with Stan having children and wanted him to have a relationship with them. His boys were ages one and twelve years old and were born by different women.

My main concern was for Stan to spend time with his children, but I wanted to know it was definitely over with the last baby mother. I wasn't sure. Stan reassured me that it was over between them.

After a while, his spending the night with me turned into him living with me. I called myself loving him, so it didn't matter what he had or didn't have. I always felt that what I want from a man has nothing to do with his finances. It does make things better, but it wasn't my focus. I was still learning when it came to guys. Stan started out working, but eventually didn't have a job. He didn't have a car either, which meant that he could end up driving my car. He had at least three strikes and I was still giving him the benefit of the doubt.

Stan sold weed and this would be his main source of income. Hustle money can never be considered guaranteed money. One day can be different from the next. Some nights he rode with a homeboy out and other nights he would ask to drive my car. Stan not having a car didn't bother me as much until he started wanting mine. He wanted to travel to his hometown and it wasn't close. Stan had a license, but I was still uncomfortable with him having my only vehicle outside of the city limits. He would leave late in the evening and would stay gone until about two or three in the morning. I really didn't mind the late nights because I wasn't working. My only wish was that he would get a job. Stan could have been up to anything while out.

Our relationship was okay for the most part. Stan's dad was extremely happy that I had taken his son in and always felt the need to repay me with very nice gifts. Stan always thought that his dad was coming on to me and this was the real reason he wanted to buy me things. Stan had gotten locked up in his hometown for a couple of months while we were together. It wasn't that long so, I didn't mind waiting on him to come home. This was around November of 2001. I wrote Stan letters and he would write me back. Our letters were filled with sweet nothings. I traveled to visit him in Lexington, NC. Stan was locked up for two months. I was ready for a change when he returned home. Things weren't the same once he returned right before Christmas in 2001. We were not on the same page and possibly never was.

Instead, he spent most of his time on the couch. Stan had it made. I felt like he was comfortable with his situation. All he wanted to do is play the Xbox and watch television every day. One thing that Stan brought to the house was a television. It was an old school floor model television, the kind that was surrounded in wood. Often, he would fall asleep on the couch. This was very annoying and arguments would arise from this. It bothered me to a point of no end. Stan would sleep on the couch through the night and I couldn't pay him to come to bed. I wanted a man that wanted to be next to me when it was time for bed. He didn't understand my reasoning.

In the meantime, Stan's dad was still buying me things such as a bed in the bag, kitchen appliances, utensils, dinnerware and etc. Everything was extremely nice and expensive. I always thanked Stan's father and told him that he didn't have to do any of those things for me. He always said that he appreciated me and the fact that I let his son live with me.

For Christmas, he got me a leather jacket and leather boots to match. Both were items I told Stan I really wanted. I'm not sure what was arranged between Stan and his father, but they made it happen. I was so happy and couldn't stop thanking Stan even though he didn't pay for anything. I wanted him to know I was thankful regardless. He made it happen no matter what.

We had our disagreements, but kept it moving. During this time, I started suggesting to Stan he needed to get a legitimate job, so that he didn't have to rely on his other lifestyle. I didn't mind him selling marijuana to a degree because we were both smoking it. I just didn't want Stan bringing anyone to the house to purchase it. Whenever someone wanted to buy some weed Stan would go to their location. Stan would keep everything locked in a safe that only he could access. I was never given a code. I should have been the least of his worries. I was still young and naïve and didn't take things serious.

Stan began searching for a job as I suggested. He would get dressed up in slacks, collar shirt and a tie, then go job hunting. He really looked nice. Even though he was looking for a job, it seemed like he wasn't. My friend Lola would be at my house during the job search. She thought that I was being too hard on him. I beg to differ because tough love is necessary. A few months passed and he got a job with Pre-Paid Legal. To me this job should have been a part-time job only and not considered full-time. It was a full-time job to Stan. This type of job was based on the people you knew with money. Some serious networking would have to take place in order to be successful. He worked with a European male who made the job look like a piece of pie! I wanted to support him, even though I felt like this job wouldn't pay any major bills. Stan was excited and ready to bring in the dough. He spent a lot of time working, but wasn't bringing any money home. It was as though he didn't have a job. Stan only wanted to play that damn Xbox 360 and talk on the phone constantly.

I've always had a temper and it didn't take much to ignite my flame. I felt like he should have been paying more attention to me when he was home, but he didn't. We got into it one day that he paid no attention to me and I flipped the kitchen table over. I didn't think twice because of my anger. I was fed up and felt as though I couldn't take it anymore.

Stan's laptop was on the table and it must have broken into a thousand pieces when it hit the floor. He was mad as hell! Stan still didn't pay me any attention. This was not the way to get him to talk to me.

However, we continued to argue. We were unable to have a decent discussion. Stan's anger lasted for the next week and I continued to apologize. The apology wasn't good enough at this point and I even offered to buy him another computer. Stan didn't want me to buy him another one. Stan didn't want anything from me at this point. I felt as though he didn't want to be bothered, at least with me. It seemed as though our relationship began to change more and more after he came home from jail. That day helped me realize what type of feelings we had or didn't have for one another. My patience with the relationship was growing thin as the relationship began to drift downhill. I didn't care anymore about my feelings or his as far as the relationship was concerned. It didn't matter to me if he wanted to work to make things better or not.

In the meantime, he was still driving my car whenever he wanted. He was still job hunting. Stan finally realized that pre-paid legal money was neither fast nor guaranteed. It just wasn't all it was cut out to be for him. He was still falling asleep on the couch in the living room after playing the Xbox 360.

I was back in cosmetology school at Carolina Beauty School on Wendover Avenue in Greensboro, NC during this time of my life. It was a different school this time around. I had to drop out of Leon's on Lee Street when Za was stalking me. I was trying my best to complete a dream. It was a dream that I could be proud of as well as my mother Bonnie. I went to school at night part-time and worked at McDonald's during the day. Stan would drop me off at school and keep the car during the 4 hours that I attended class. He would come to pick me up around 9 at night. I wanted his butt outside after my class was over. Some nights he wouldn't be there on time to get me. I had no idea what he was up to when he dropped me off. It didn't matter. I wanted Stan back to get me on time once class was over. Sometimes, after class he would keep me waiting. Stan would be doing other things that were obviously more important than me.

One night Stan dropped me off at school and I wouldn't have imagined the outcome. I had a test that night and I was running over my usual time. He came to get me. Stan decided to leave my school and go back to where ever he was. The nerve of him. The whole time I was thinking that he was outside waiting for me to finish up. I even called to let him know that it wouldn't be that much longer and I would be out soon.

My instructors were ready to leave after the test, but had to wait on his return. All the students had left and my instructors didn't want to leave me in an empty parking lot alone. He embarrassed me! My instructors had to wait with me on my ride, which happened to be my car. The class ended at 9:00 p.m. Stan got there at 9:30 p.m. I was heated beyond control by the time he arrived. I stayed calm until I got in the car with him and actually left the school premises.

I had just purchased some popcorn from the school's vending machine and was still munching on it. I just couldn't figure out what was so damn important that he couldn't wait. The messed up part is that he didn't see anything wrong with his actions. I was so mad at the fact that I had to call Stan about my own car. I was going off on him and throwing popcorn all over the car to show my frustration. I was screaming at the top of my lungs with disgust. I let him know this was the final straw and that I couldn't take any more. Stan was selling drugs, driving my car around to do it and not working on top of everything. I felt like he chose his homeboys or whoever he was with over me.

I already felt like he didn't give a damn about me and tonight the truth was shown. I told him that I wanted him out tonight. I had been good to Stan and he had given me nothing, but his black ass to kiss. Everything had been on me. Not anymore. A part of me thought that I was making the wrong decision, but I followed through with my instinct. I called Stan's father and told him what happened. His father had to drive from Lexington. It took about an hour and a half for him to get there. He brought the truck over to get Stan's personal belongings. He apologized, and continued to apologize that it had to come to this. Overall, he said that he understood.

We remained friends after that night. We would talk every now and then, but he was still upset. He was upset about how we broke up and it showed. All I could think about was the fact he really didn't love me in the first place. The more I tried to talk to him, the more he turned his back and treated me like dirt. We were together for a year and half.

When I love, I love with all my heart. I wanted to end the relationship and after ending it, I thought I wanted him back. I was actually just comfortable with him being around me and didn't want to start over with anyone. The two of us were really better off apart. I began feeling better about the break-up and thankful that he didn't want to get back with me. I was able to grow and Stan helped my growth through our separation. I was able to reflect on the good and bad points of myself. I needed self-reflection more than anything else. A man would only block this energy. I felt like I needed him, but I really didn't. Stan was going to be the one missing out on a very good woman. I know now that he didn't deserve me. I let my anger get the best of me. Stan wasn't worthy of what I had to offer.

I learned a valuable lesson about relationships after that one. You can't make someone love you if they don't. We all tend to believe that we can make someone love us. No actions or anything you do for someone will make them love you. A person loves you or they don't and have no problem showing you. When the relationship is over, let it be and don't cross that bridge again. It took me awhile to get over him because I thought I really loved Stan. The reality of the matter was that I had reached a comfort level with him and that's totally different from true love.

I moved on and became stronger. Each relationship gives you the positive and negative in life that you can reflect on. My future was bright and I didn't have time to dwell on the past. I finished cosmetology school about five months later. The graduation was held at the Greensboro Coliseum and only a handful of family and friends showed up, if that. I didn't let it discourage me because I had goals to accomplish. I hadn't taken the state board for my cosmetology license because I really didn't have anyone that would take me. It was in Lenoir, North Carolina. The fact that no one offered to take me bothered me. I thought to myself, if they didn't show up for my graduation. I doubt they would take me to complete the state board hours away. This is the one time that I felt my family wasn't there for me.

My passion for hair came from growing up around my mother doing hair. My mother Bonnie was fabulous at doing hair. Styling hair came quite natural to her. She passed that gift on to me. The last salon my mother worked at was the JC Penny Salon. It was in the Carolina Circle Mall in Greensboro. Bonnie found out that she had breast cancer. JC Penny's offered her a management position at the salon. Sadly, she had to turn the position down due to her failing health. She was known for doing hair very well. My mother Bonnie had a strong passion for hair and by me owning a salon. It would be like me living out her dream. This has always been my motivation to own a salon. I knew my mother would have had her own salon by now.

I wanted to own a beauty salon. My plan is to own a salon one day. It's my heart's desire! Whenever I stopped working at a salon, I would style hair on the side at home. I was fortunate to attend Leon's Beauty School which was the same beauty college that my mother attended. I didn't know if I was more ecstatic about going to school or learning in the identical environment as my mother. Some of the instructors remembered my mother and was happy to meet me.

While attending Leon's Beauty School, my mother's long time friend came back to school. Her name was

Robyn. Robyn reminded me so much of my mother. They had similar hair styles, close in height, light skinned women and loved red lipstick. This was crazy! It was like Robyn and my mother Bonnie were in school all over again together. Between Leon's and Robyn, I felt extremely close to my mother's spirit. Life seemed to be moving in the right direction for me.

I knew a man that grew up with my family. Richard owned a salon called Flashlight. I didn't need a license as long as I worked as an apprentice under someone that was licensed. I began working at Flashlight's immediately. I started building my clientele base. I worked at the salon part-time. I didn't stay there long because life happened and other things got in the way. I went from working at Flashlight's to taking calls at InfoNXX. InfoNXX is a call center. The salon business wasn't going as I had expected. I wasn't making the desired money. I needed more income to survive. Every time I attempted to work in a salon, bad things would happen! My license was stolen off of the wall at Flashlight's. No one saw anything!

My relationship with Stan was over. It was over and Stan was nothing like Brad. I was fooled. I thought that Stan could be what I needed. Stan wasn't. It took me a year to move on from Stan. I was officially living the "single life!" I began to hang out more. Friends were still hanging out at my place. I was 24 with no kids, single, a car and had my own place. I could do whatever. I had no one to answer to about anything. I knew that I wanted to date. I needed to date with caution because of Stan.

I met a guy that worked for a company that distributed hair products. Ja'ron was his name. His sister and I stayed in the same apartment complex. Ja'ron stood five-foot-nine. Ja'ron was 27 years old. He had a brown sugar complexion, a close haircut with an average texture of hair. Ja'ron's body had some definition and there was no flab. He was in shape. Ja'ron would work out from time to time at the gym. Ja'ron approached me while I was in the parking lot to my apartment complex. We exchanged numbers. There was nothing that I couldn't ask for when it came to hair products.

Ja'ron worked at Hair Mart which was a supply store. Ja'ron was the driver for Hair Mart. He distributed the products to the different hair salons. I would get a delivery either once a week or bi-weekly. Ja'ron would come to my apartment in the company van and I would stock up. The second bedroom had more shelving than any other room. It was perfect for all of my hair supplies. My closet was so stocked that I could be a distributor. I really liked Ja'ron. He was a hard working legal guy which I wasn't used to.

It was something about him. Ja'ron seemed to be involved with another female. I couldn't quite put my finger on it. Eventually, I figured out he was talking to me and another girl. We were friends with benefits. I was angry and wasn't sure why. Ja'ron and the other female were even more serious with their relationship than ours.

One day I decided that I would follow Ja'ron to his destination. He drove to A & T State University which wasn't far from my apartment. Ja'ron parked in front of the college library. Ja'ron appeared to be waiting on someone because he didn't get out of his vehicle. After waiting for 20 minutes, a female walked out of the bookstore and got into the jeep with him. I couldn't wait to speak with Ja'ron and tell him that he was busted. I felt betrayed. I called Ja'ron when I got home. I informed him that I saw him with a female. I finally had proof and it couldn't be denied. This would be the end of our fling. Ja'ron admitted that the female was his children's mother. He didn't try and dispute me being right!

This was enough for me to move on no matter how much he sweet talked me. When someone is dishonest with me and I have to end up pulling the truth out, then it's best to let it go. If a man has been caught being dishonest to you with someone else, he will think that he can do it again if you stay with him. He will think that it's acceptable, but not with me. I wasn't about to stand for it, so I separated myself from him. We needed to end this now, so that we could be friends at the least or it was going to get ugly.

As time progressed, he ended up marrying the female that he was dishonest on me with. The messed up part is that his new wife had no idea that her new husband had feelings for another woman. I had mixed feelings about the situation because I still cared for Ja'ron, but I was more upset about his dishonesty. I was more disappointed in the lies and the betrayal placed upon me. Ja'ron told me that he had feelings for me and even loved me, but married another woman. It didn't make any sense to me and I wasn't going to be naïve.

I learned a valuable lesson from this encounter. There were signs in the beginning that I chose to ignore. Ja'ron didn't discuss meeting his family or take me around them. He obviously had something to hide. A woman should be cautious of a man that doesn't invite her to his home. Women should be careful when a man can only spend a limited amount of time with her. This includes spending time with their children. Everyone should be interacting after the relationship is supposed to be serious. At some point in life, you don't want to snoop and you shouldn't have to. When you have to search for secrets the relationship isn't solid. There's nothing to stand on and it's a complete waste of time. The old saying "what's done in the dark will come to light", is very true. Please don't be a fool for anybody. The dirt always surfaces no matter who is

doing it!

Atlanta

Once I left Ja'ron alone, I was back to a place that seemed to be the best. Single! This allowed me to enjoy my family and friends more. I went on dates with guys and to the movies. I even took trips whenever I felt like it. I always liked going out. I never had a problem meeting new people. I would always leave my apartment and car with someone in my family. I'm not materialistic. Those things can be replaced. Layla, Nya and my brother Travis would normally hang out at my place while I was out of town. Whenever I was in Atlanta, nothing else mattered back home. Everything was paid for. I was basically vacationing with no worries.

My Nissan Sentra had seen better days. It was still my baby. I was in Atlanta one particular time. Nya called to tell me what had happened. Nya and her boyfriend Will were trapped in my car. I had no idea what to tell her to do. I had never heard of such a thing. There wasn't too much that I could do being two states away. Nya knew not to lock the doors on my car. If you did the window needed to be down. Just to reach your arm out and open the door from the outside. Everyone knew except Nya's boyfriend. They ended up being locked in the car. I'm not talking about for a few minutes either. It was for a couple of hours in the Four Seasons Mall parking lot. I had an idea. Nya had different people trying to open the car door, but couldn't. I told Nya to break the window. I would replace it later. As crazy as it sounds, that was the best option. The police had already been called by the security guards at the mall. The policeman told them to cover their heads while he wrapped his arm in a towel and broke the window. They were able to escape from the car. Nya's boyfriend learned to never do that again.

Whenever, I visited Lola in Atlanta. We would get dressed fly & sexy then head out to the club. The nightlife in Atlanta was popping! We always had something to do. It was nothing to meet someone famous. Atlanta was more exciting than the night life back home. I looked forward to the option to go somewhere every night. Every night there was a new experience at a different club.

One night Lola and I went to Club Vision's. We hung out in the parking lot. We didn't want to go inside the club that night. I had a man's attention. He was standing outside of his car and we were sitting inside Lola's car. She was driving her mother's black 96 Pontiac Grand Am during this time. He was close enough to speak with me and I spoke back. I ended up getting out of the car to move a little closer to him. We introduced ourselves to each other and he told me his name was Shawn. He was 37 years old. Shawn was six-foot-four, a pecan brown complexion, wore corn row braids and his clothing was relaxed. The shoes that he had on literally looked like house shoes, but were expensive. Shawn wore them to the club.

Shawn wasn't feeling the club either. He asked if we wanted to go back to his house. Lola and I decided to follow Shawn to his home. Shawn asked me to ride with him before getting in the car with Lola. Lola edged me on to ride with Shawn. I grabbed my purse and decided to ride with him. Shawn was driving a black 2001 Mercedes s550 with chrome rims and tinted windows. His car was new with all the bells and whistles. I wouldn't have guessed that Shawn smoked, but he did. Shawn asked me if I knew how to roll. I rolled up the blunt and it was on from there. We smoked during the drive on interstate 95 to his house. When we arrived at his house it was a mansion. Wow! It was gorgeous! I held my composure and wouldn't dare show my awe. On our way into his house, Lola kept whispering to me, "Who have you met girl? Who have you met?" I said, "I don't know," and kept walking. I didn't want talking to Lola to blow my cool. I was acting as though it didn't faze me, and this wasn't the first mansion I had visited.

Shawn's home was three levels with a three car garage, swimming pool, and the backyard was gated. The garage had other vehicles inside of it. The basement had a movie theater, a pool table and another huge bedroom with a nice size bathroom. The second floor consisted of the kitchen, dining room, living room, den and his private office. His office was definitely private. We chilled there while getting to know one another. The living room had a bookcase that was built into the wall. It was covered with plaques and trophies that reflected his scholar achievements while playing in the NFL. The third floor was where the five bedrooms and three bathrooms were located. His home and especially his bedroom was the exact rendition of MTV's Cribs. Shawn had more shoes than one could count along with his clothing. The master bedroom had an additional room where his personal gym was located. Shawn had some workout equipment there. There was a small room with a love seat and an enclosed balcony decorated with patio furniture. Of course the master bathroom was the size of a small house. The bathroom was humongous with a shower and a bathtub. Not to mention his and hers sinks.

We eventually found out that I had met a retired NFL player. Shawn Maynard played for the Chicago Bears and now lived in Atlanta, GA. I was blown away and couldn't believe it. I always heard about the things that took place in Atlanta. I was actually living it!

Shawn and I immediately hit it off. I was invited back to his home whenever I visited. We spent time relaxing by the pool and drinking wine. Shawn always invited me to the parties he promoted.

Lola and I would get in free. V.I.P. was a must! V.I.P. consisted of the people that were spending money. V.I.P. stands for very important person. Normally, V.I.P. is a private area in the club and cost more to enter. It was a must that we chill there. V.I.P. was the place to be once you stepped foot in any club, especially in big cities. I would mingle and guys would buy me drinks. I had always heard that you shouldn't have a drink that you didn't see made.

A guy named Nate was trying to kick it with me and wanted me to leave from the club with him. Nate had no idea who had invited me to the party. Shawn already had dibs on me. Shawn told us to come to his place after the club was over and there would be no passing that up. I already knew that I was leaving with Lola. We were going to spend the night. Shawn had a friend that lived in the basement along with other guys just stopping by. Shawn's friend that lived with him liked Lola. Shawn's place was the spot to chill on the weekends.

So, Nate brought me a drink and I didn't think twice about it. Nate was so iced out. He had ice all around his neck, wrist, on his ear and finger's. All of his jewelry was shining ridiculously. It was blinding. I began drinking the drink that Nate had made for me. It wasn't long before I began telling Lola I had to go to the bathroom. It wasn't because I had to use it either.

The clubs in Atlanta stay open until about six in the morning. It was getting late. I had planned to be there until closing, since it was Shawn's party. I mentioned to Lola that I was going to the bathroom. I went to the bathroom around 3:00 a.m. Lola began worrying about me. I hadn't returned yet. I heard her calling my name in fright upon entrance of the bathroom. I was laid out on the bathroom floor. This was something that I had seen other drunken females do in the club. I thought it was disgusting. Now I understand there's no control in the matter. The only difference with me was that I had been officially slipped a "Mickey". A Mickey is a drug that is slipped into a drink to take advantage of people. It's the worst thing that could ever happen to anyone. I let Lola know what I felt had happened with me and she said", that bastard! Lola would curse someone out in a minute. She didn't care about their feelings. She asked me who he was and I explained. Lola remembered exactly who he was, but he had disappeared by now. There weren't many people left in the club all together.

There was nothing that could be done. The club was closed now. It was around 5:00 a.m. I had been in the bathroom for such a long time that everyone had left. Shawn had begun to wonder where I was as well. Shawn had taken care of his business and was ready to leave. However, a good amount of time had gone by while I was passed out on the bathroom floor inside the stall. It was somewhere between one and two hours. I immediately knew something was wrong with that drink. It acted on my body so fast. Lola brought me some paper towels wet with cold water. I mustered up the strength to get up off the nasty floor and splash my face with cold water. Once outside in the fresh air, I felt better. I was happy to have people around me that cared.

Everyone's body is different when it comes to a controlled substance. A man can take advantage of a woman in this type of situation. I knew never to take a drink from anyone else again. If I didn't see it come from the bartender. I don't need it. Before I went to the bathroom, I had already exchanged numbers with the guy that slipped me a Mickey. He never called me to find out where I had disappeared to, which was strange since he wanted me to leave with him. I waited until I got back to North Carolina and called him. I asked him about slipping that Mickey in my drink. Of course he denied every bit of it. I cursed his ass out! Just for lying to me and putting me in harm's way then hung up on him. That feeling is like no other and it's recognizable. It doesn't take long to realize something is out of the ordinary with your body. Shawn and I remained friends. We kept in touch by phone, but as time went on, we eventually lost contact. Shawn changed his number and it was years before we connected again.

Each trip to Atlanta was interesting. On my next visit, I kicked it with Hahns. He was a guy that I met in Atlanta when I first started hanging out there. Hahn's was six-foot-one, light skinned with black curly hair and thick eyebrows. He was 30 years old. Hahn's looked as though he could have been a model. He told me when we first met that he used to be a pimp. I told him that it was no way. Hahn's seemed too young to be a pimp. I didn't believe him. I thought he was fine enough to be one. Hahn's didn't have his shit together. He had someone in his life outside of me. Hahn's said he was finished with the lifestyle as a pimp. I was his side chick that he claimed he wanted to make his main. Hahn's gave me the talk as if he really didn't want to be with his girlfriend. We all know how that conversation goes and how most guys act when they want to get into your panties. We could only be friends. Hahn's seemed to be cool with that. We were the friends with benefits. I had someone in North Carolina that liked me a lot. I stayed in Atlanta a couple of weeks and returned to Greensboro. I wasn't ready for a commitment with anyone.

Carl was a heavyset guy, brown skin, wore corn row braids and stood about five-foot-ten. He was 34 years old and dressed casual. My Nissan Sentra was broken down and I walked to the store. I met Carl and he began helping me out. He made sure I was okay. I didn't want a relationship with Carl and he knew this.

He had grown on me over time. I liked him and didn't want to hurt him no matter what. Carl would do absolutely anything for me that I asked of him. He was a nice guy. He had someone in his life, but told me he wanted to be with me. Carl was down for whatever made me happy.

During the spring of 2001, I told him that I wanted to go out of town for my birthday. Carl gave me $500 for a trip to Atlanta for a week. He purchased me a rental for the week and I hit the road. When I arrived in Atlanta, I went to stay with my friend Lola. I planned on seeing Hahn's during my week-long visit. I had already filled Hahns in about Carl. I told Hahn's all that Carl would do for me. There would be no talk of letting Carl go.

Hahns understood because he had a girlfriend. Carl had big plans for me while I was away. My best friend Deon knew that Carl was planning a surprise while I was away. I didn't know anything. Carl was purchasing a car for me. Meanwhile, I'm hanging out with Hahns and doing it up in Atlanta. Hahns didn't have a lot of money to begin with. I ran out of money and Carl asked me how much more did I need. He sent me more money through Western Union. At that instance, it seemed that life couldn't get any sweeter.

One night, Hahns and I spent some time together during my stay. It was normal for us to see one another whenever I visited. Hahns and his girlfriend lived together, but that didn't stop him. I went to pick him up in my rental car. We had an unexpected discussion sitting in the apartment complex parking lot. It was the same complex that he shared with his girlfriend. The conversation we had made everything spiral out of control. Hahns began to tell me that he wanted to be with me. He wanted to come back to North Carolina to live with me. Everything happened so fast that I couldn't digest it. I knew that I didn't want Hahn's coming to Greensboro just to live off me.

All of a sudden something came over him. Hahn's showed me another side. A side that was dark and cold-hearted. He told me that he needed to use my phone. I gave him my pink Nokia flip phone and didn't think twice about it. I had no idea that he really made a call. I never saw him put the phone to his ear. Hahn's looked in my phone and dialed Carl's number allowing him to listen to the entire conversation. It was the conversation that Hahns was having with me.

At this point, Carl knew everything that I had been doing in Atlanta. I couldn't deny any of it because it was as though I dialed his number purposely. This was the lowest thing that Hahns could have done to anyone, especially me. I had officially broken Carl's heart and I felt extremely terrible. I didn't even want to face Carl once I returned home. Carl told me that he would be returning the car that he purchased for me. It was going to be a surprise gift for my upcoming birthday. I thought he was just talking to make me feel even worse, but it was true. Carl really had purchased me a brand new vehicle. Deon told me that he had seen the small jeep. Carl wanted to get me a car. Carl knew that my car was older and I really needed a dependable one. This was the sweetest thing that anyone had ever done for me and I blew it.

Everything was over between us now. We remained friends. Carl wanted us to try and work our friendship out. He liked me as more than a friend. We didn't need to cross that road. I thought it was best to keep a platonic relationship. We would talk from time to time. Carl always wanted to check on me. Hahns and I remained friends, but nothing more. He still wanted to move to North Carolina with me. I would be the only person he knew. I would be responsible for transportation and helping him get a job. No matter how upset he was, I couldn't take on this task. Most importantly, Hahn's had did me wrong with Carl.

I met someone by the name of Fránc at the Club Stroker's in Atlanta. I met Fránc during my week-long stay with Lola. Fránc was in his early forties, medium-size build and a dark complexion. He was a distinguished gentleman that dressed in suits. Stroker's was one of the most popular strip club's in Atlanta. It was nothing to party with the stars.

One night, T.I. and Tiny were there with their entourage. Tiny was sitting on T.I.'s lap most of the night. It took me a few months to call Fránc. He remembered exactly who I was. It was after the incident with Carl. I was home in Greensboro at this time. We talked on the phone a little. We talked long enough to arrange to see one another. Fránc offered me a round trip ticket to come and visit him.

It was the summer of 2002. I jumped at the idea of a free trip to Atlanta, so we planned it. This was a place I always enjoyed visiting. I was guaranteed to meet someone and already knew people there. I arrived at the airport and Fránc awaited my landing.

Once in the Cadillac SUV with Fránc, I noticed that he spoke more than one language. Fránc immediately began making phone calls. It seemed he wanted to inform everyone that I was there. When Fránc got off the phone, I asked him if he was speaking French. Fránc answered yes and told me that he could speak a total of 4 languages. This took me by surprise. I wasn't ready for it. It meant that Fránc could be saying anything about me and I wouldn't know it. This wasn't my first time being around a man that spoke a different language. It was my first time being out of town with one. We continued down 85 South to a restaurant where we met with one of his friends whom spoke one of his languages. After having dinner, we began to head to his home. Fránc had already mentioned to me that he had lots of women's clothing. Fránc wanted me to try on some of the outfits. I didn't realize what level this man was on, but it was major.

Fránc's home was a long one level brick home in a suburban area. It was a ranch style home that was spacious in both length and width. The furniture was a mixture of antique and modern. The layout had a gothic feel to it. The decorations were elaborate and placed very well. The entrance consisted of two doors as though you were entering a palace. They were made of a very solid and expensive wood. You could open either side or both doors at the very same time.

Once we entered the threshold. Fránc closed the door. I noticed the door had several bolt locks, at least five. Fránc locked every last one of the locks one by one. Fránc made his gun visible to me. I was shocked that he would even think to show me a weapon. I didn't ask any questions. I acted as if it didn't bother me. We were in his home and I looked around cautiously. I wanted him to lead the way, after what I had already witnessed. I would only take a step if he took one or directed me to. After giving me a peep here and a peep there we took a seat in the living room.

We sat down to talk about our plans for the night. I noticed what appeared to be a money tree. Literally, there was a money tree with money at the base of it. I had never seen a real live money tree in a person's home. It was sitting in the corner of his formal living room area. I asked him the purpose of the tree. Fránc said that when people entered his home they must drop money there in order to visit him. I didn't think twice. I went into my purse. I found a one dollar bill and placed it at the bottom of the tree as everyone else had. I wanted to make this visit as smooth as possible. Fránc then showed me to the room where I would be staying. I began changing into the outfit of my choice after searching through the wide variety. We

would go out on the town after I was
ready.

Fránc wasn't exaggerating when he
told me that he had women's clothing.
There were two closets filled with
designer clothing and shoes. It was as
though I had entered a high end boutique.
The outfit that I picked out was one that I
wanted to keep by Azure. It was a popular
brand and didn't come cheap. The outfit
was so hot! I even had high heels of my
choice to match everything. I couldn't
wear the heels. The shoe size was smaller
than my feet. I had to wear a pair of my
shoes that I had brought along. I didn't
want to because they really didn't match
my stylish outfit. I made it work though.
This was a lot for me to take in. I had

never come across anyone like Fránc. The jeans had stylish rips in them and the top was sleeveless with the same design as the jeans. It showed some skin, not too much. I couldn't quite get a feel for Fránc, but I knew he didn't play. Fránc had already told me that I couldn't keep the outfit, and once the night was over, it must be returned. I didn't mind.

Now that I was getting dressed, I wanted some privacy. I didn't really talk to any of my friends at this point in my life that lived in Atlanta. I still had their numbers. I did call Hahns. I told him that I was in town. I wanted to call a couple of people that lived in Atlanta to let them know of my whereabouts. Just in case I needed someone to come to my rescue. I went in the bathroom and realized that neither the bedroom nor the bathroom had locks. Fránc could burst in on me whenever he wanted. I didn't like that. My eyes went from the door to the window. They were locked down with bars.

I called Hahns back and described my environment to him. I even told him Fránc's name. Hahns told me that he knew exactly who Fránc was. He was one of the biggest pimps on the East Coast. Fránc never mentioned that he was a pimp to me. Hahns suggested that I get out of there right away and as safely as I could. My conversation was brief with Hahns and besides I didn't want Fránc to hear me on the phone. I was frightened after hearing such a thing. This explained all the locks on the front door, the locks not on the bedroom door and the bars on the windows. I knew that Fránc and I were going back out. We had planned to hang out, so I would think of something. I finished getting dressed and remained calm. I didn't want to let on to what I knew about him. Fránc was getting dressed in his bedroom.

About an hour had passed and Fránc said that he was ready to go. We went to the Huddle House to meet his friend for conversation. Fránc had arranged for me to leave with his friend that came to meet us at the Huddle House. I had no idea what was about to take place. The Huddle House is a breakfast spot in the south. It has the same resemblance as the Waffle House. I went into the bathroom to call Hahns and inform him of my location. I continued to play it off until Hahns had arrived. It took Hahns about 30 minutes to arrive because he was waiting for me to call.

When I spotted Hahns, I informed Fránc that I was leaving and my ride was here for me. He was bothered, but it was nothing that he could do. Fránc said okay and told me to take his clothes off. I had my travel bag with my personal belongings. I changed into my clothes. I handed Fránc his clothes and thanked him for everything. I was so happy that I had someone in Aţlanta to get me out of a situation that could have turned out to be the worse for me.

Hahns took me to the track that night. The track is where females work at for pimps. He wanted to show me where the girls worked at for him when he was a pimp. It was true; he really had been a pimp. The girls showed him love and respect. Eventually, Hahn's and I lost contact with one another. That was my last excursion to Atlanta. It shook me up. I didn't even want to be seen or contacted by Fránc again. I started spending more time in North Carolina.

Felonies

There were many people in my hometown that I knew and whom knew me. I attended one of the most popular high schools in the city. James B. Dudley Senior High School was the only all black public school in Greensboro. Dudley was number one on the list and Smith High School was second on the list as being the most popular school in the city to attend. My personality wouldn't allow me to meet a stranger. I only had a select few in my circle. Sometimes I would hang out with other people that were friends of my friends. When you're young, you just want to have fun. Most people don't have your best interest at heart, but it has to be learned. Okay, this is not a good choice when it comes to the company you keep!

I was 25 years old at this time and always kept my friends close. Every now and then I would associate with mutual friends. I really didn't choose the best associates to surround myself. Which assisted with my poor choices. I didn't think twice about their intentions. I was only concerned about the now. Which consisted of doing drugs, partying and living life to the fullest. The people I chose to hang out with were what you would call entrepreneurs of the streets. Everything they did was on their own time and didn't have to answer to anybody. I hung out with people who didn't mind spending money. They wanted everyone to know that they had it like that. It didn't take long for them to make the money back. I dealt with guys who owned houses, drove any car they chose and didn't have to wear the same outfit twice. We would eat out every day if we wanted to and at any restaurant we chose. It was nothing for me to ask for money and get it. I along with my girls' always met guys like this that wanted to show off what they had. They showed off by spending money.

The city that I'm from is not the biggest. Neither is it the smallest. If you don't know someone then you probably heard of them. That's how it is in Greensboro. Everybody knows everybody. I knew what guys were ballers and players. A baller is a person that spends plenty of money. A player is someone that has many women. Greensboro is considered country, so it wasn't hard to recognize the shot callers. Every since I was a teenager, a part of me always felt rebellious in nature. This is what attracted me to the bad guys or at least the ones participating in the pharmaceutical street life.

There was a store called John's Curb Market on East Market Street. People would hang outside of the store. It was a place that I would visit frequently for gas. I would go there several times a week and a few times throughout the day. I was guaranteed to run into someone. Most were people that I already knew and others were always trying to talk at me. I traded my Nissan Sentra for a 2001 Dodge Neon. I could use some help on my car payment. I was approached by two guys that I had never seen before. Their names were Reece and Quinn. We all were in desperate need and could use help in a major way. It was in May of 2002. They needed a ride to Baltimore, Maryland and I needed some money for my car note. I was told I could make up to $500. We would stay the night and return the next day. Reece and Quinn needed someone to take them to pick up some drugs. What type of drugs? I didn't know. It sounded perfect to me. I really didn't think twice.

Lola was in town that weekend. I asked Lola to ride with me and she said no. She didn't want to ride with two strange men 4 hours away. I had no idea where we were headed and what they're true intentions were. I told them to give me about an hour and I would meet them back at John's. I kept my word. I grabbed a few things from my place and picked them up at John's. We headed to Baltimore. This was my first drug run. I wanted my car note paid when it was all said and done. I didn't have to reach in my pocket for anything on our way there. They paid for food, gas and the room. We smoked weed and talked while traveling to Baltimore.

We arrived in downtown Baltimore close to midnight. I was nervous the entire time. A part of me believed that I was safe. They purchased a hotel room for the night. It was a hole in a wall and the least expensive hotel. The plan was to stay the night and leave after checkout in the morning. I would have never thought the strangers whom I picked up would be gentlemen. They were and even allowed me to sleep in the bed while they slept on the floor. Neither one of them tried anything with me. Things went according to plan and we left the next morning. We arrived at a Baltimore project where we would be picking up the drugs. The streets consisted of children playing unattended and teenagers talking in groups. I could see drug deals taking place right before my eyes. The police were patrolling the area, but kept driving as though they didn't see it. The guys left me in the car alone and went to handle their business. I locked the doors as I waited on their return.

They came back to the car and we were back on the highway to Greensboro. It was that simple. I never asked any questions. Once back we entered their apartment on Church Street called Lexington Commons. I went to use the bathroom and when I came back to the living room I was surprised as to what I seen. They dumped a garbage bag of pills on the coffee table. It was covered and I had no idea how much it was worth. I helped transport ecstasy and was happy

just to make it home safely. I was paid
$400. I took the money and thanked them.
I went on my way and never looked back.
We never crossed paths again. I didn't
keep the Dodge Neon and purchased
another white Nissan Sentra.

I wanted to talk to the guys who
had money to blow and wasn't working
the 9-5. I knew so many people and chose
to surround myself with the guys that
hustled. These surroundings influenced
me. I thought that it would be easy for me
to hustle and make fast money as well. It
seemed as though I could get away with it.
I didn't think that I would be as noticeable
because I was a female. I wouldn't be
suspected as a drug dealer. It had always
been a secret thought of mine. I wondered

what it would be like to be in the "game".
In a sense, I was already in the game, but I
wasn't the provider. I was strictly the
buyer who used the drugs. I wanted to
use the expensive drugs only. The entire
time I never thought that I could get in
any trouble just being around it. I could
get a charge from that alone.

As time went on, my girl friends and
I were on the party scene with the guys
and getting it in! My girl, Lola, met a guy
that hustled and she liked him. His name
was Raheem. Raheem was 26 years old
and five-foot-nine. He had dreads, a
brown complexion and brown eyes. He
wore baggy jeans; white t-shirts and fitted
hats. Lola liked him and Raheem liked
her. They began spending a good amount

of time together. They're good amount of time was usually spent at my house. Raheem would give us money and drugs whenever he came around, so we really enjoyed his company. He seemed to be a cool cat from what we could see.

Lola was from Greensboro, but moved to Atlanta, Georgia after high school. Lola would come to visit periodically. Normally, she would stay at my house. Raheem had gotten cool enough with me that I began to let him come over when Lola wasn't in town. Nothing was going on with us, but the way he came over would make you think otherwise. It didn't matter what anyone thought. I knew it was strictly business. The business part happened so fast with

Raheem that I didn't even realize it. I looked at him as a homeboy that was mad cool that wanted to look out for a sister with no strings attached. This was far from being true.

During this time, I was really being naïve to what was really taking place. That's when I knew what this life was about. Things were moving fast. Things started to move so fast that it made my head spin. Raheem asked me if he could start cooking up his product at my house. I had never seen crack cooked in such a large amount. No guy in the streets had ever approached me about anything like this. A part of me was really afraid of allowing it. Another part of me thought it would be cool. I didn't think too much of it because I had never been in any drug related trouble. I felt like I wasn't hot and wasn't known for hustling. This should be smooth sailing. I told him to let me know when he wanted to start. This would soon become a decision I would never forget.

My cousin Nya was living with me at the time due to some issues at home with her step-mother. Nya was 16 years old with long black hair, a pretty brown complexion and petite. My Uncle Butch asked me a couple of months prior about Nya staying with me. My Uncle Butch gave me money monthly to help with the bills during Nya's stay. Nya's visit would be temporary and I told my uncle that I was okay with it. This was cool with me because I had the living space. I was now responsible for her. I had to take her to school and pick her up. I was 25 years old and basically taking care of my younger cousin. We also had our differences at times because she didn't want anyone to tell her what to do.

I understood Nya. She reminded me of myself when I was her age. I only wanted to listen to my mother and Nya was going through the same thing. Nya didn't want anyone to discipline her and would become upset if anyone tried. This was the issue between Nya and her step-mother. We would always get over our differences and overall I could tolerate her. I gave her space and had conversations about the reality of life with her and what to expect. I didn't keep secrets from Nya and made sure we had an open relationship. I wanted Nya to be able to talk to me about anything that concerned her. However, with this being said, she couldn't know about everything. I told her about the birds and the bees. I didn't tell Nya about the drug life. She couldn't have known how deep her older cousin was involved.

I didn't mind if Nya knew about me smoking weed, but not anything harder than that. My Uncle Butch would go crazy if he knew that I had his little girl in this type of environment. I wanted to be a positive role model to Nya as much as possible. I wanted to show her the things to do and not to do. I had all of this in mind and somehow felt that I could keep it from her.

Raheem told me he was ready to start cooking his product. I would tell Nya to stay in her room whenever Raheem came over. I would tell her that I would let her know when she could come out. She would ask me questions like, "why do I have to shut her door and what are you doing". Nya wanted to know who was in the house. Nya was smart and knew that something wasn't right about what was taking place. Raheem would come over for about an hour to cook his dope. It would smell and even sounded like someone was literally cooking in the kitchen. I'm not sure if Nya smelled it or not and I never asked her.

The timing was perfect because there was a drought. A drought in the streets is known as a lack of drugs. It was 2003 and practically no one had any type of drugs. I decided to become a female kingpin. Many that needed anything would come my way. The streets were butt naked. The suppliers that normally held the weight didn't have any. There was a rumor that the drought would last for months. No one that normally had the work knew when they would get more. I was one of the few people that had the cocaine and the marijuana. People were doing any and everything to locate an ounce of weed.

It was October of 2002, the weekend of A & T State University's

Homecoming. A very good amount of money from within the city limits was entering my hands. The money was there, pockets were fat compared to what I had. We didn't have to spend a dime unless we wanted to. Whenever we were with the entrepreneurs of the street. Needless to say, I became busier than I ever imagined.

Raheem would be cooking dope and I would be right by his side taking notes. This process of cooking dope amazed me. I would watch in awe. It was such a large quantity that deep inside, I felt nervous and even scared at times. I was nervous about the police. It seemed the police could bust the door down in search of Raheem or the activity. Raheem would be at the oven. I would look on while getting high on drugs. While in the kitchen, I would make sure I kept everything clean. The process of cooking dope was messy. I had to keep a fragrance going to cover the smell.

Honestly, this was the most drugs that I had ever laid eyes on in my life. Things began racing through my head like, from where did Raheem get this amount of drugs from? What was his motive for wanting to befriend me? I often wondered why Raheem had chosen me? The reason why my home was best to do his dirty work? No matter my thoughts, I continued to let him cook his dope at my house. I wasn't thinking correctly anyway due to the drugs and money involved. I could see no evil. I wanted to get high on Raheem's drugs. I was so fascinated with the idea that I could become "big time". This life seemed to be glitz and glamor from the outside looking in.

Before Raheem came along, I already owned a gun. I had a gun permit due to the incident with Za. Raheem knew about my gun and asked me if I would keep some guns for him. This was supposed to be a favor, on top of the other favor I was already allowing. The first favor should have been enough. I was still clueless to the amount of trouble that I could face. The guns could have been stolen, or even have had a body on them. A body meaning that he could have murdered someone. I had no idea. I didn't dwell on it. I wondered where the guns were coming from. I told him that he could bring them over anyway. Raheem brought two guns over. I now had possession of three guns all together. I thought to myself that he must have someone else to keep them. Why me? I figured that he must have someone else in his life closer than me. He had to have known someone longer than me whom he trusted. Regardless, I went along with the stupidity.

Everything that I was allowing to take place happened very fast. Right before my eyes and without warning! I had become part of the biggest type of organized crime. My house was now a dope house whether I liked it or not.

Raheem was cooking up the crack in my kitchen. My friends, along with me were getting high on Raheem's marijuana. We were being satisfied.

Eventually, Raheem had someone meeting him at my house to count money on the kitchen table. The drugs and money involved was no less than $60,000 at every encounter with this distinguished black gentleman. He looked to be in his mid-forties. I don't remember his name, but he had a suspicious look about himself. He wore glasses and dressed in a casual manner. Not in the street gear that Raheem wore. He traveled from Raleigh, NC each time to meet with Raheem. I continued with this escapade that unseeingly at the time was spiraling out of control. I allowed it because I could get free cocaine and marijuana. The drugs were important to me in a way that led me to making more poor choices. Raheem also allowed me to get a discount on excessive amounts of weed. I had to save my money in order to get a pound of weed. I could get a pound of weed for $600 from Raheem. It was easy and I was able to save my money in no time due to the drought.

Now I realize that I should have been getting them at no charge. Raheem should have been really paying me! However, I was green and did everything that he suggested in his favor. I really wasn't gaining because I didn't realize that he wasn't on my side. I knew the game was dirty, but didn't recognize it even when it stared me in the face. I should have been getting more money as well, but it didn't work out like that. Raheem appeared to have it going on as though he was the man in the streets. In actuality, he was getting this huge amount from someone else. It's called "fronted" when you get the product and pay later. This was what Raheem was doing and he really wasn't the man.

It was January 2003. I remember as if it was yesterday. I decided to call it a night early rather than a late one. I wanted to go to bed early after taking a bubble bath by candle light. All I wanted was to relax and not be disturbed by anything or anyone. While taking my bubble bath, the telephone rang. I picked the phone up and someone told me that they needed something from me. I didn't mind making this sell because it was right around the corner. He needed some white. I would get back home in no time. I planned on shutting everything down for the night. I was ready to have a date with me, myself and I doing whatever made me happy. My bath was so relaxing and I had been looking forward to it all day. I had the candles going along with some party favors while in the bathtub. I was getting right by myself and enjoying every minute of it. I wasn't in a rush to get out even after taking the phone call that involved money.

After that call, my telephone started ringing again. This time it was Raheem. He shouldn't have been calling me at this time of night. It had only been a couple of hours since he left and he asked if I was still up. I told him yeah and he said that he needed to come over. Raheem had been over earlier that night for business and didn't mention coming back. I could honestly tell in his voice that something wasn't right with him.

Something was definitely going on, but I couldn't figure out what. He called once and then another call came a few minutes later. It sounded like he was at a party during the second call. Raheem asked me to open the door. I asked him where was he at? So I could open the door and he is there. Raheem told me that he was across the hall from me and they were having a party. He had used someone's cell phone at the party. I didn't even know a party was going on that night. I never heard any music outside of my door. I only heard the music in the background during the phone call. This dude never told me that he knew anyone in my building. I told him to give me a minute because I was in the bathtub. I put my robe on and went to the door to find Raheem standing there already.

I opened the door and there Raheem stood just as awkward as he could possibly appear. I let him in and began to ask questions. I wanted to know what was going on with him. What was the reason for his strange ass behavior? It was about midnight and Raheem came over unannounced. I didn't appreciate it and wanted him gone immediately.

Earlier that day, Raheem came over and did his thing. I hadn't even cleaned the kitchen up after he had left. I had a long day. Raheem being there was one of the reasons's I wanted to go to bed early. I was frustrated at this point with the whole scenario. First of all, Raheem claimed to be at the neighbor's party across the breezeway. I couldn't even hear any music and the apartment is diagonally across the hall from me. That bothered me something terrible. Secondly, I had no idea that he associated with anyone that close to me that would let him come into their home. Thirdly, why in the hell was he sweating profusely and sounding as if he was out of breath?

All of the above things had me frantic. This situation came out of the clear blue sky. It was far from my mind. I had been relaxing in my bubble bath for the past thirty minutes and bam it was over! My relaxation was out the window now due to his shenanigans.

Raheem needed to explain everything that was going on with him and wasn't talking fast enough for me. We were standing in the living room and didn't move to sit down or nothing. Raheem started to explain to me what was going on. This dude tells me that he was in a high-speed chase due to him running a red light on Martin Luther King Drive. I know I'm not the only one in the area that he knows. Immediately, a light went off in my head. I'm wondering what the real reason was that he ran to my house. Raheem said he wasn't far from my house and had nowhere else to go. All of this sounded like garbage to me. I wasn't buying any of it.

Raheem claimed that he threw his phone and that's why he had to use the neighbor's phone the second time he called. Okay, but who would let a stranger in to use their cell phone. I heard the music in the background while we were talking, but I didn't hear it when I answered the door. Raheem should have stayed at the neighbor's house. He said

that he had a key of dope in the car.
Raheem had to throw it out the window
while driving.

On top of everything he had already
told me. Raheem claimed that he ran from
the car into the party to call me. The
whole time he was telling me the story I
knew it was fishy. It was beginning to
smell. I just wasn't sure exactly what he
was conjuring up. Everything was moving
so fast that I still didn't have time to apply
any logic to what was about to go down. If
all of that happened, the police should
have been so close to his ass that he
would have never made it to my door!

Raheem was sweating like someone
who had stolen something or like the
police was after him. The sweat never

stopped rolling down his face while he was explaining to me what had happened. I'm not saying that he shouldn't have been, considering all that he said he had been through. With the high-speed chase and him getting rid of the cocaine.

Something just didn't seem right to me! There was nothing that he could tell me that would make me believe the crap! I couldn't believe what Raheem was kicking as he stood in my living room. When he finished telling me the story, Raheem told me that he needed a ride somewhere. He had been really fast talking to me. My head was spinning at this point and I just said okay. I told him to give me a minute and let me change clothes real quick. I still had to go around the corner to the person's house that called me while I was taking a bath.

The entire time Raheem stood in the same spot telling me some bull crap. It took about fifteen minute's total, but it seemed like an hour had passed. I never took time to look out the window or even the front door for that matter. I never heard any police sirens or any type of commotion when the police supposedly chased him into my apartment complex. I went to my bedroom and got dressed. I needed to prepare to make my run and drop his ass off as soon as possible! I wanted him away from me. He had interrupted me and I didn't appreciate it.

Nya was in her room with the door closed and unaware of the chaos that was unfolding. She was awake, but was talking on the phone like most teens her age. I let her know that I was about to drop Raheem off and make a run. Everything was close to my home and I planned to come right back. However, that wasn't the case because I had no idea what was in store for me. There was more for me than I could have imagined once I stepped foot outside of the front door. Low and behold, I was far from coming right back.

My apartment was located on the second floor on the front side of the building. I remember how the scene in front of my house looked just like it was yesterday. Raheem and I came out of my apartment and I locked the door. I was still unaware of my surroundings. As I started walking down the stairs toward the parking lot, I noticed several police cars. The Greensboro Police Department were in the parking area and had surrounded the apartment complex. Some were still sitting inside their police cars and some were on foot. They were only around the building I lived in. This was extremely strange to me and with no warning. I continued in their direction because I knew this wasn't for me. The police were positioned at the bottom of the stairs along with their K-9s.

I had never seen anything like it and most definitely had never been involved with anything this bizarre. Right away, I knew it was all over Raheem. I was in just as much trouble because I was with him.

His explanation in my house was only the beginning to the drama. This picture didn't look good at all. I was in shock and couldn't talk if I wanted to. I immediately felt that I had been trapped and there was no way out. We reached the bottom of the steps and the police started approaching us. They were asking questions about the individual for whom they were looking for. They wanted to know if we knew anything. I had no answers for them and continued to walk. I didn't stop and walked right past them as though they weren't talking to me.

Raheem stopped like an idiot and talked to them. I didn't care what he was doing and I continued to my car. I wondered why in the hell Raheem's dumb ass stopped to talk with them. He was the person of interest. You mean to tell me that you were on a high-speed chase from the police and now you want to have a conversation with them. Please! You have got to be kidding me! Raheem should have pulled over when the lights were chasing after him. He might as well turn himself in and stop playing around.

Once in my car, I started my car and drove off the premises. I didn't even warm up the car. It was cold outside too. I left Raheem standing there with the police. A part of me wanted to know what lies he could possibly be telling the police. I kept driving. I drove as if there were no police in sight. My heart dropped earlier when I reached the bottom of the stairs. I knew this was bigger than I had ever imagined. I was embarrassed and didn't want my neighbors to see me going through this. That's the main reason I drove off. The other reason was to get rid of the drugs I had on me. I tossed the crack out of the driver side window and kept driving. It was a small amount. Regardless, I didn't want it on me.

I left Raheem and this made the situation look even worse. It made it look like I was part of the whole thing. Nothing mattered at this moment. I wasn't able to drive too far because the police began to trail me as I attempted to leave the apartment complex. That was good enough for me as long as I wasn't in the spotlight of my neighbors.

The police followed me closely with their blue lights spinning behind me. It seemed like every police car in Greensboro was at my apartment complex on Willow Road. They wanted Raheem and he was seen walking out of my house. This was the most outrageous thing that I had ever experienced in life. I made it onto Willow Road and pulled over to face the music.

While, I was driving from my apartment complex, I called Nya to let her know that the apartment was surrounded and not to let anyone in. I asked her to try and get rid of any paraphernalia that she could find. I wanted Nya to dump the ash trays and wipe the kitchen cabinets down. That would be helpful. Even though it was no way that it would physically be possible. There was evidence all around the apartment. I had a few friends over the previous night and we had been up all night. Raheem had been over earlier this evening and it was evident. The trash can was full of vacuum seal bags that Raheem used. The pots that Raheem cooked the dope in were dirty and in the kitchen sink with residue on them. Nya told me how scared she was of the police. I told her that everything was going to be alright. Deep inside, I was just as terrified on the other end of the phone. I didn't want Nya to know.

I called Lola to let her know what was going on and that it looked like I was headed to jail for the night. Next, I called my cousin Layla to inform her of what was about to happen to me. I've always been able to count on Layla. I wanted to tell more than one person what was going on with me or at least what I thought was going on.

I was pretty sure that I was going to be in jail for the night. I didn't know if I needed someone to get me out or what. I had no idea what was going to happen to me next and to what extent it would be. I knew that I didn't want anything to do with Raheem after he had gotten me into this mess. I definitely didn't have too much to say to him either. Overall, I knew no one could help me at this point.

The police got out of their car and started to approach my vehicle. I was scared. By this time, I was crying hysterically. The tears wouldn't help, but my emotions were raging. I told the policeman I had nothing to do with Raheem and whatever he had done. The police asked me if Raheem was my boyfriend. They said that he told them that I was his girlfriend. I said "no," I'm not his girlfriend and I met him through a mutual friend. Even though it seemed that we were more than friends. It was strictly business. Nothing sexual. It was more than one cop harassing me now. I told them that Raheem asked me for a ride and that's what I was doing with him. Whatever I said at this point didn't matter to them because the entire GPD had witnessed us leaving my home together.

They wanted me as well and there was no getting around it.

I was eventually read my rights and you already know your fate once that happens. Before the police put me in the police car, I resisted arrest. I wanted some justice because I felt that I had been violated and set up. The police threw me down on the ground and mace me as well before I finally gave in. I had no choice. After the mace was sprayed into my eyes, it seemed like I was going to hyperventilate. I was out of breath after the tussle and bustle with the cops. I kept taking deep breaths because I thought that I was going to literally pass out. This was my first experience with mace and it was horrible. With all that I was going through a part of me wanted to be non-existent.

At this point anything would have been better than my reality. Now that I was in the back of the police car. I was wondering how I would tell my family about all of the trouble I was in. There was no way that my family would believe that I was involved with anyone of this nature. I didn't know how to explain making a poor choice once again. I was terrified. I didn't know where to begin whenever it came time for me to face my family. My life would change forever, from this point on and I had no clue to what degree.

When I arrived at the police station, we entered through a garage that was only for police officers and bail bondsmen. The garage was dark and creepy looking. The lights were so dim that it appeared as though no lights were on. I arrived at the jail at midnight. The handcuffs were extremely tight and were removed once I was inside of the jail. The police took me straight to the water fountain. The fountain wasn't a regular fountain either. It was made specifically for eye rinsing. I was directed to the fountain to rinse my eyes out due to the mace. The water was supposed to ease the burning of my eyes. Unfortunately, this really didn't help my eyes and the burning would have to wear off over time. No water was going to take away the intense burning sensation that made me not want to open my eyes at all.

After rinsing my eyes out, I was told to sit on the bench because a police officer was coming to talk with me shortly. The cops knew that I was of no threat and therefore it was no need to place me in a cell. I was given my one phone call while in holding. The officer that came to talk to me was trying to force information out of me. I didn't have any information or even know what this was about. The police wanted me to answer all of his questions. He told me that I would get a lesser charge for talking and he would tell the judge I cooperated. Normally, this is the time when you "snitch". While, I was in holding, they brought the real "snitch" in. Raheem. He was placed in a cell unlike me. Raheem put his finger to his mouth and told me to ssshhhh. Whatever that was supposed to mean. Raheem was still playing and taking this as a joke. He was familiar with trouble. I wasn't concerned about keeping quite about anything that could help him out of his mess. He had some nerve even thinking that I was his ride or die chick. Raheem had the wrong one. Raheem was the one that needed to get to talking and not me.

The police wanted me to cooperate by allowing them back into my house on that very same night. I knew nothing about the system during this time, just that I was scared as hell! I wanted everything to be finished. The police told me that it wouldn't be that bad if I did what they asked of me. It really didn't matter if I cooperated or not because I was going to be punished regardless. That was one thing I knew for sure if I knew nothing else. The only thing on my mind was to get out of jail as soon as possible. The police and I went back and forth and then I decided to let them into my house. This was my only hope because there was nothing to tell the police. Everything they wanted to hear would need to come from Raheem.

I was put in the back of the police car to be driven back to my apartment. This time it was without the handcuffs. This was part of the deal that would give me leniency with the judge and would allow me to get out the same night. I had no idea that it didn't matter if I let them into my house. It would have been best for me to stay in jail for the night. I didn't know that I would have been better off letting the police get a warrant to search my place. I made it easy for the police and in the end they didn't do anything for me. The police played me as well. It benefited them only.

Once we were at my place, I unlocked the door and was told by the police what my next move should be. They gave me instructions on what to locate and bring to the living room. First, I was told to get the weapons. They wanted the fire arms visible and in a particular area. Secondly, I was told to show them where any narcotics were located. I had a pound of marijuana and $200 cash in my place that night. Third, I was told to sit on the bed and not to move until the search was over. Nya had to come out of the bedroom and sit with me in the living room. The search was very intense and lasted for hours. My place was torn to pieces unnecessarily, even though I was supposedly "cooperating" with them.

I can't even remember everything that was racing through my mind at the time. I was thinking more about the next day, explaining this devastating news to my family and friends. I was out of it at this point. I wasn't looking into the future and had no idea how hard my life would be. I was such a good, intelligent and hard-working girl with goals. I wanted so much for myself and my life.

Now! No matter how smart I was, my name would be put in the system as a criminal. At this point, the police had pulled the insulation out of my attic in the master bedroom. The insulation had fallen into all of my shoes that were in my master bedroom closet. It was on my clothes and the floor.

My house was a disaster! I didn't know that letting them in would have the same turn out as a warrant. I had a lot to clean up after the search. On top of everything, I would now lose my beautiful apartment that I loved. A drug conviction on the property leads right to an eviction. This conviction would also terminate what help I was getting from the system. My life was about to be two times as hard as it already was. Things were about to get real!

After the police finished the search, I was taken back to the jail house. The search lasted until 3:00 a.m. The magistrate allowed me to sign myself out after everything was over. I was given my paperwork with all 7 Felonies. Lola and Nya came to get me from jail. Nya was driving Lola around that morning. We went to McDonald's on Summit Avenue which was open 24 hours. We went to one of our home boy's house named Owen to talk with him about all that I had been through. We smoked weed while we were over there. Owen kept asking about Raheem and there was nothing that I could tell him. We left once the sun began to come up. I couldn't sleep even if I wanted to. Lola came in once we got back to my place. Nya was still with us. The police could have arrested her or removed her from my custody, but they didn't. I was thankful for that. The three of us stayed up all morning with no desire to sleep. I was stressed about my life now.

All I wanted to do was get high all morning while talking about Raheem. He had set me up to take the fall for someone else's drama and I couldn't get over it.

Later that same day I told my family and they absolutely couldn't believe what they were hearing. They wondered what would make me get involved with this type of situation. I wanted to be honest with them. My family has always been my biggest supporters and I didn't want to cut any corners. I needed them while going through the lowest and most degrading ordeal in my life. My family never judges me. They stayed by my side and thought I made a poor choice, but as long as I learned the lesson from it. My family didn't mind helping me. I had to call on everyone. Not just my family, but friends as well. Anyone that could help me out financially would be needed. This case would cost me a lot to walk on the streets and avoid doing any time.

Once that night was finally over, I would have to face a harsh reality about my life. I would have it harder than ever before. It would be a difficult transition for me mentally. I would have to get use to rejection and hearing "no" when applying for jobs. When it came down to looking for a job, my education would no longer outweigh my criminal record. Meaning I would have to put forth more effort than the average person to prove my skills.

Now, whenever an employer ran my criminal back ground check for employment, a long arrest record with charges would follow. My record would now show 7 Felonies that would portray my image in a whole new light. My 1st charge was possession of marijuana, 2nd was possession with intent to sell and distribute marijuana, 3rd was the manufacture of cocaine, 4th was maintaining a vehicle dwelling place, 5th was trafficking cocaine, 6th was manufacture of marijuana, 7th was possession with intent to sell and distribute cocaine.

All 7 Felonies would show a false reality of who Shapell Depree really is as a person. Some of the charges didn't even belong to me. I had to wear the charges associated with Raheem. The key of cocaine was found at my apartment complex. The key of dope that Raheem supposedly threw out of his window. When drugs are found on your property, you become the owner. This was the perfect scenario to make the police assume that Raheem and I were really partners in the game. It all started three months before, and my life ended up in a complete nightmare. If I could have ever had the chance to do things differently, this would have been the perfect time or reason.

I had to come up with a lot of money that I didn't have and wasn't sure if my family did. This was for my attorney fees and retainer. This case had to go to court and was my only hope for not spending any time behind bars. My Grandfather Billy Brooks was living at this time, but died later in 2003. My grandfather suggested I go to Joe and Bruce to discuss my case. Joe and Bruce are attorneys in Greensboro, NC. My family on both sides knew Joe and thought this would be best for me. I didn't want to have anything to do with Raheem no matter how much money he claimed he would give. My family advised me not to as well. Especially, being that they were going to help me get the money together.

Raheem contacted me a couple of times. I didn't want to talk to him, but I wanted to hear what was on his mind. He insisted that we meet and talk in person. I didn't think this was the right thing to do because we didn't need to be seen together. I wanted to look at him in his eyes and read his body language, in person. I wanted to see if I got the same vibe from him. Raheem claimed that he wanted to give me some money to help with my lawyer fees as well. He knew that I didn't have any money and that this would sound good to me.

I met Raheem to get the money, only to find out that he wanted me to continue to hustle. That was out! I didn't want any parts of that life. I was already in trouble and didn't need anymore. Raheem seemed to still be trying to set me up or pin something on anyone that would allow it. It wasn't going to be me again. This proved more than ever that he didn't give a damn about me or my outcome in the case. Afterwards, I cut all ties. I strictly relied on my family and friends to help me. Raheem meant me no good, and it seemed that he wanted me in prison with him. Raheem had been grimy from the very start and I knew it now, but didn't stick with my intuition. This situation can happen to anybody, but it sure doesn't have to. It's not worth messing up your life.

I had to give up a place that I adored. I moved back to the side of town that I was raised on. The town homes were called McKnight Mill on Sixteenth Street. It had two bedrooms, one bathroom upstairs and the other half bathroom was downstairs in the laundry room. It had an awkward layout, but this would be my home for now. This was a huge change from the place I had loved at first sight. My cousin Nya was still living with me. I continued to take her back and forth to school each day. My uncle believed that I had learned my lesson and was comfortable with Nya continuing to live with me. My brother Travis would come and stay over some nights. I didn't feel as safe in this apartment, so I was always happy whenever my brother stayed.

I was sentenced to three years' probation, community service and court fees. Some forms of probation require drug testing. My probation was supervised and I had to report monthly. I had to be tested once a month for three years. The drug testing steered me away from doing drugs as much. I had to complete 120 hours of community service. My taxes due to Uncle Sam were in the amount of $60,000. The money owed was the street value equivalent to a key of cocaine. Over a three month period of time, the street value of the drugs in my presence was near $200,000. Raheem was sentenced to 2 years in prison.

Even though I didn't get any prison time, I still felt like I was trapped. I felt like I was a prisoner in my own mind because of my limitations. I wanted to make the fast money, but my old ways had to be out the window. I knew that if I got in anymore drug related trouble, I would definitely do time. There would be no second chance.

This situation has helped me realize why most drug dealers continue to sell. Once you have been in trouble, it's hard to find a job. You need money so you do what has become familiar. If I knew nothing else, I knew that I didn't want this type of lifestyle. I had to make better choices. I had been through so much in my life before this situation. I couldn't help feeling like I had been cursed for something and I had no idea why. I was so thankful for the outcome, yet mad as hell at my self for the poor choices that I had to live with.

The part that hurt me the most was not being able to get a job! I was qualified and could pass any test given. Once the employer did the background check. I could hang it up! I remember the first time I applied for a position. The question was asked if I had been convicted of a felony. I had to check yes or no. I contemplated on whether to be honest or not. I checked yes and finished the application. The temporary agency called me and said that I didn't have a record. They wanted to know my reason for checking yes and told me nothing had come back on my record. Still being honest, I told the lady that I have a record. She said she would check into it more and call me back. She called me back after about an hour. She told me that my name had been spelled differently in the system when I was arrested. Therefore, it didn't match my license and the background check gave me a clear record.

When the lady called me back to inform me of the mix up, I pleaded. I asked her not to report the different spelling of my name, but she did. I felt like I had a second chance. In that moment, if I would have been dishonest. I beat myself up about that for quite a while. I would no longer be able to get a job that paid the amount of money that it takes to survive. Thank goodness for the struggles previously in my life. Those struggles prepared me for the road ahead. It would be an even harder journey through life, but I was ready!

My family kept asking me if I could get the charges expunged. I inquired about the steps for expungement. When I asked my lawyer about expungement, he told me that it wasn't possible. He then suggested that I work for myself. That had always been one of my goals. I didn't want it to be solely because of my background. My family really didn't want to believe that there was nothing that could be done.

My family wanted to come up with money that they didn't have just to expunge the charges. They would do anything to make my life better. They wanted me to be successful. Those thoughts alone meant the world to me.

My strength along with my faith was being tested daily. I had to stay positive. I had to keep telling myself that what the most high has for me is for me. I had to believe that someone in the workforce would give me a "second chance" at a career. I continued to feel as though I had it rough.

My life from the outside seemed as though everything was together. If people only knew how I wished it was. I continued to put applications in at different jobs. I had previously worked for InfoNXX. A call center in McCleansville, NC. Eventually, I heard they didn't do background checks and was hiring. I left in good standing and this allowed me the opportunity at employment. I went to put in an application right away. I passed all tests as usual. I was hired without the background check. I was on my way to getting my life on the right track. The legal way!

Epilogue

We never know what angle that life will come at us, but I have learned to be aware of my surroundings at all times after this situation. My mindset is different now and I no longer want to be in the game or be a part of it. My mission is to help women of all ages become aware and conscious of their environment. If your record is clean, be sure not to let the ignorance of someone else change your life forever. Ultimately, most individuals don't want to listen and have to learn it on their own. The hard way. I'm a walking testimony that people care about themselves more when it comes to getting out of trouble. Remember that no man is worth jeopardizing your future. I don't regret anything that has happened to me because I've learned from my mistakes. What happened in my life has happened for a reason. It was a huge eye opener for me and allowed me to view my life more cautiously.

This particular situation and even the ones before it taught me to appreciate my life along with myself. I began to desire a life that I had never imagined before. My ambition in life became stronger and I actually sat down to analyze my goals. I took time to write my goals out and actually plan. We all go through different scenarios to help prepare us for our future. I think before I act and understand that there are consequences. The things we learn will apply later in life and when you're young you don't even realize the significance of poor choices. The correlation comes later in life. My current situation had me thinking about college when before I didn't think that it was for me. It just wasn't for me at that time in my life. I now have aspirations and goals toward the betterment of my entire well being.

Everyone has a divine purpose on Earth. You just have to be willing to find it. Individually, we have different times when things are revealed and significant to you only. The creator allows an intervention with the reality of our life on his timing.

Out of all of my trials and tribulations, I must say that the 7 Felonies are the most enlightening of my life experiences. The path of my life has prepared me for encounters and experiences that I can't even imagine. No matter what obstacles you encounter, they all have unique lessons that you can apply to your life. In the end, my future accomplishments will shine brighter than my past!